A DECADE OF ACHIEVEMENT

1860-1960 PONY EXPRESS

Harriet Tubman

Black Heritage USA 13c

WHO'S GOT MAIL?

The History of Mail in America

AFRICAN ELEPHANT HERD

NAISMITH 1861-1961

LINDA BARRETT OSBORNE

ABRAMS BOOKS FOR YOUNG READERS ★ NEW YORK

FOR
CATHERINE, NICK, AND MARY KATE,
LOVERS OF HISTORY,

AND FOR
JIM WAUGH,
FRIEND, MENTOR, AND LETTER WRITER EXTRAORDINAIRE, WHO TAUGHT ME TO READ BEYOND THE LINES

First Class Mail® Priority Mail®, Priority Mail Express®, and USPS®
are registered trademarks of United States Postal Service.

All stamps courtesy of the National Postal Museum, Smithsonian Institution.

Cataloging-in-Publication Data has been applied for
and may be obtained from the Library of Congress.

ISBN 978-1-4197-5896-6

Text © 2023 Linda Barrett Osborne
Edited by Howard W. Reeves
Book design by Sara Corbett

Printed and bound in China
10 9 8 7 6 5 4 3 2 1

ABRAMS The Art of Books
195 Broadway, New York, NY 10007
abramsbooks.com

CONTENTS

INTRODUCTION

Vernon O. Lytle, mail carrier on rural route No. 5, is the first man to accept and deliver under parcel post conditions a live baby. The baby, a boy weighing $10\frac{3}{4}$ pounds, just within the 11 pound weight limit, is the child of Mr. and Mrs. Jesse Beagle of Glen Este. The boy was well wrapped and ready for "mailing" when the carrier received him to-day. Mr. Lytle delivered the boy safely at the address on the card attached, that of the boy's grandmother, Mrs. Louis Beagle . . . The postage was fifteen cents and the parcel was insured for $50. —*New York Times*, January 26, 1913

The Post Office soon put a stop to this practice after several small children had been mailed to save the price of a train ticket. But while there are a few things it won't deliver—most alcoholic drinks and explosives are forbidden—it has carried everything from abolition literature to sewing machines to live baby chicks. The history of postal service in America goes back more than 250 years.

IN 1900, A MAIL CARRIER POSES WITH A TODDLER IN HIS DELIVERY BAG. ALTHOUGH THIS PHOTOGRAPH WAS TAKEN AS A JOKE, AFTER PARCEL POST SERVICE WAS INTRODUCED IN 1913, AT LEAST TWO CHILDREN WERE MAILED TO RELATIVES. THEY TRAVELED BY RAILWAY MAIL SERVICE.

Even before the American Revolution, the British colonial post, supervised by Benjamin Franklin, was transporting letters and newspapers. Increasingly these supported independence for the thirteen colonies. Franklin was fired by the British for his efforts, but the new American government made him its first postmaster general. Franklin and the other Founding Fathers, like George Washington and James Madison, believed in the need to keep all Americans informed about their government through an effective postal system.

Post Office history is America's history. It is a sweeping story of how a federal institution helped the nation grow. The Post Office extended transportation and communication to the most remote places in the country. Congress requires it to deliver mail to every American, no matter how expensive it is to reach far-flung homes and businesses. In 2022, the Post Office was still using mules to deliver mail to the Havasupai Indians at the bottom of the Grand Canyon. Ten to twenty-two mules, depending on the size of the load, travel nine miles into the canyon six days a week. It takes three hours to descend and five hours to climb back up. Delivering to everyone is the main mission that has shaped the service's entire history.

The U.S. Constitution mandates a Post Office Department in article 1, section 8. It is Congress's job "to establish Post Offices and post Roads." Congress passed the Post Office Act, establishing postal routes, in 1792. As the United States grew, the Post Office grew with it. It moved west with pioneers, traders, and fortune hunters. By 1801, when the United States was only twenty-five years old, postal routes stretched for 21,000 miles and the young American government had established 903 post offices.

MULES CARRY U.S. MAIL TO THE HAVASUPAI INDIANS WHO LIVE AT THE BOTTOM OF THE GRAND CANYON. DELIVERY TO THE SUPAI POST OFFICE BEGAN IN THE 1930S. SUPAI HAS A SPECIAL POSTMARK SHOWING A MULE TRAIN.

Wherever the Post Office went, it improved or established roads that not only allowed quicker passage for the mail but that everyone could use. Its work was vital to building the young country's transportation system. "[The mail] is to the body politic what the veins and arteries are to the natural [body]—conveying rapidly and regularly, to the remotest parts of the system, correct information of the operations of government, and bringing back to it the wishes and feelings of the people," said President Andrew Jackson in 1829.

Since it goes everywhere, the Post Office has been creative in inventing ways to deliver the mail. "Here on a sledge

made of whalebone, drawn by a team of domesticated reindeer, Uncle Sam's postman hurried over the trackless snow-covered tundras," according to the *Chicago Tribune* in 1909

REINDEER TRANSPORTING MAIL ON SLEDS IN 1909. THEY CARRIED MAIL TO MORE THAN A DOZEN POST OFFICES IN ALASKA, INCLUDING SEVERAL NORTH OF THE ARCTIC CIRCLE. THEY WERE USED UNTIL SOMETIME IN THE 1910S.

A FRENCHMAN PRAISES THE U.S. MAIL

The early Post Office's reach was so extensive it impressed foreign visitors. "I traveled along a portion of the frontier of the United States [in Michigan] in a sort of cart, which was termed the mail," wrote the Frenchman Alexis de Tocqueville in the 1830s. "Day and night we passed with great rapidity along the roads, which were scarcely marked out through

of one route in Alaska. In 2022, in a tradition that started more than one hundred years ago, carriers were still jumping from mail boats to the docks on Lake Geneva in Wisconsin.

The United States Postal Service (USPS) is one of the country's largest employers. More than 516,500 people worked for it in 2021. It is especially known for the

A TEENAGE EMPLOYEE WHO WORKS FOR THE CRUISE LINE JUMPS FROM A PASSENGER-CARRYING, PRIVATELY OWNED MAIL BOAT TO THE DOCK. SHE CARRIES MAIL FOR THE SHOREFRONT RESIDENTS OF LAKE GENEVA, WISCONSIN. THE TRADITION STARTED IN 1916 BECAUSE ROADS WERE TOO DIFFICULT TO TRAVEL. THE SERVICE RUNS FROM MAY TO SEPTEMBER EVERY YEAR.

immense forests. When the gloom of the woods became impenetrable, the driver lighted branches of pine, and we journeyed along by the light they cast. From time to time we came to a hut in the midst of the forest; this was a post-office. The mail dropped an enormous bundle of letters at the door of this isolated dwelling, and we pursued our way at full gallop, leaving the inhabitants of the neighboring log houses to send for their share of the treasure."

diversity of its workforce. "Minorities comprise 52 percent and women comprise 47 percent of the total workforce," according to USPS's Annual Report in 2021. Of these, about 29 percent were Black workers, 13 percent were Hispanic, and 8 percent were Asian American. "The Postal Service is also a leading employer of veterans with approximately 10% of its workforce comprised of veterans, nearly double the national average employment rate. It is more diverse than the U.S. labor force as a whole."

GUESS WHO HAS WORKED FOR THE POST OFFICE

Many Americans (with the exception of Benjamin Franklin) started working for the Post Office when they were young, before they forged their careers and became famous.

★ Founding Father **Benjamin Franklin** was the first postmaster general of the United States.

★ Future presidents **Abraham Lincoln** and **Harry Truman** served as postmasters: Lincoln in New Salem, Illinois, and Truman in Grandview, Missouri. Truman's appointment turned out to be honorary, since he gave the running of the post office to a widow who needed the work. Future president **William McKinley** was a mail clerk near Poland, Ohio.

From its beginnings, the postal workforce made speedy delivery in all conditions a top priority. When the main post office building in New York City was completed in 1914, its facade displayed these words: "Neither snow nor rain nor heat nor gloom of night stays these couriers from the swift completion of their appointed rounds." It was inspired by the mission of ancient Persian messengers, who traveled by horseback more than 2,500 years ago. "Nothing mortal

★ **John Brown**, the abolitionist who attacked Harpers Ferry, was the postmaster in Randolph, Pennsylvania.

★ Author **Richard Wright** (*Native Son*) was a substitute clerk in Chicago. Novelist **William Faulkner** (*Absalom, Absalom!*), winner of the Nobel Prize in Literature, was postmaster for the University of Mississippi.

★ **Walt Disney**, creator of the entertainment conglomerate, worked as a substitute letter carrier in Chicago.

RICHARD WRIGHT WAS A POSTAL CLERK IN CHICAGO IN 1927, BEFORE HE MOVED TO NEW YORK CITY. THERE HE WROTE THE GROUNDBREAKING 1940 NOVEL *NATIVE SON*. IT PORTRAYED AFRICAN AMERICANS IN A REALISTIC WAY THAT WAS NEW TO WHITE READERS. HIS AUTOBIOGRAPHY, *BLACK BOY* (1945), DESCRIBED WHAT IT WAS LIKE TO GROW UP IN THE SEGREGATED SOUTH.

★ Actors **Steve Carell** (letter carrier, Littleton, Massachusetts), **Bing Crosby** (clerk, Spokane, Washington), **Rock Hudson** (substitute letter carrier, Winnetka, Illinois), and **Sherman Hemsley**, star of the television show *The Jeffersons* (clerk, Philadelphia and New York City), all worked for the Post Office as young men.

★ Aviator **Charles Lindbergh** was an airmail pilot.

★ Swimmer **Shirley Babashoff**, twice an Olympic gold medalist, was a mail carrier in Huntington Beach, California.

★ Singer and Grammy Award winner **Brittany Howard** was a rural carrier assistant in Alabama.

★ Grammy Award winner **John Prine** carried mail in suburban Chicago. The title of his live album, released in 2011, was *The Singing Mailman Delivers*.

travels so fast as these Persian messengers," wrote the Greek historian Herodotus in the middle of the fifth century BCE. "[T]hese men will not be hindered from accomplishing at their best speed the distance which they have to go, either by snow, or rain, or heat, or by darkness of night."

In the twenty-first century, the Post Office has not lived up to its popular slogan. Delivery is not as efficient or timely as it once was. Since the later part of the twentieth century,

★ Singer and songwriter **Freddie Gorman** served as a letter carrier in Detroit for several years. He cowrote "Please Mr. Postman" for Motown Records. "I ran into [songwriter] Brian Holland who was working on a tune one day that [singer] Georgia Dobbins had suggested a title for," Gorman said. "She'd come up with the title 'Please Mr Postman' so, with me working at the post office, it was very easy for me to write the lyrics. I just used things that happened to me carrying mail."

FREDDIE GORMAN WAS A MAIL CARRIER IN DETROIT WHEN HE WROTE THE LYRICS FOR THE HIT MOTOWN SONG "PLEASE MR. POSTMAN." SHOWN HERE IN 1969, HE ALSO SANG WITH THE VOCAL GROUP THE ORIGINALS. IN 2006, "PLEASE MR. POSTMAN" WAS INDUCTED INTO THE SONGWRITERS HALL OF FAME.

ONCE NEW YORK CITY'S MAIN POST OFFICE, THE JAMES FARLEY BUILDING ON EIGHTH AVENUE WAS CONSTRUCTED BETWEEN 1911 AND 1914. IT BEARS THE INSCRIPTION, PARTLY SHOWN HERE, "NEITHER SNOW NOR RAIN NOR HEAT NOR GLOOM OF NIGHT STAYS THESE COURIERS FROM THE SWIFT COMPLETION OF THEIR APPOINTED ROUNDS."

Congress has debated whether the service should change and how it should be run.

But government criticism of the Post Office is not new. There have always been some members of Congress who complain about the cost of supporting it. In 1870, some wanted to raise the price of stamps to bring in more money. Massachusetts senator Charles Sumner pointed out that poorer Americans would not be able to afford an increase in price. He asked the Senate why the Post Office should be expected to make money at all. It was mandated by the Constitution, just like the Army, Navy, Treasury, and other departments. Yet the Army, Navy, and Treasury were not asked to fund themselves.

"There is nothing which is not helped by the Post Office," Sumner declared. ". . . I insist that . . . the Post Office shall be admitted to equality with all other departments of the Government, so that it may discharge its own peculiar and many-sided duties without being compelled to find in itself the means of support."

In general, the public loves the U.S. Postal Service. In a national survey in 2020, 91 percent of Americans viewed it favorably. Even in the age of the internet, they depend on it for, among other things, the delivery of medicine, Social Security checks, income tax refunds, and packages of every kind. Beginning in 2022, it rose to the challenge of delivering free in-home COVID-19 tests provided by the government to every American who requested one. Rural people, older people, and poorer people especially need a service they can afford. Private delivery companies like Federal Express (FedEx) and United Parcel Service

"THERE IS NOTHING WHICH IS NOT HELPED BY THE POST OFFICE," CHARLES SUMNER DECLARED IN 1870. EIGHTY YEARS LATER, IN 1950, THIS CARRIER BRAVES SNOWY WEATHER TO MAKE SURE THE MAIL IS DELIVERED ON TIME.

(UPS) are not interested in traveling to remote places, and they are generally more expensive to use.

Congress has argued about who should finance the postal service—and even whether it should remain part of the federal government. In 1970, it passed the Postal Reorganization Act, with the goal of cutting costs.

AMONG THE AVAILABLE JOBS IN THE 21ST-CENTURY POSTAL SERVICE

★ Postmasters of a post office facility, whether large or small, who manage all the affairs of the office

★ City and rural mail carriers, who deliver mail to individual addresses

★ Window clerks, who sell stamps and take in packages at post offices

★ Mail processors, who sort the mail as it comes in

A WINDOW CLERK IS READY TO PROVIDE MAIL SERVICE IN EUREKA, UTAH, IN 1996. SHE HAS ONE OF THE MANY KINDS OF JOBS HELD BY USPS WORKERS.

★ Mail handlers, who load and unload mailbags and packages

★ Motor vehicle operators and mechanics, who work with USPS's fleet of trucks

★ Custodians, who care for facilities

This was the first major change to the way the service operated since the eighteenth century. The Post Office was no longer totally a government organization, part of the president's cabinet and funded by Congress. The reorganized postal service now runs as a combination of government and private business.

Until 1970, the postal service was known as the U.S. Post Office Department. It was often just called the "Post Office," as it is referred to in this book. After 1970, its name was changed to the United States Postal Service (USPS). When talking about the last fifty years or so, this book uses the term "USPS." Sometimes the text covers the entire period of postal history. Then the general term "postal service" is used.

The postmaster general is the person in the top postal position. Until 1970, he or she was appointed directly by the president of the United States. Today the postmaster general is appointed by a nine-member board of governors. Since the president appoints the board of governors, he does have influence over the choice of postmaster general. The Postal Regulatory Commission sets postal rates.

Who's Got Mail? explores the history of the Post Office and how it became the institution it is today.

1
EXPANDING WITH THE NEW COUNTRY

I n the spring of 1763, Benjamin Franklin hit the road. As postmaster general of the American colonies for the British government, he was dedicated to improving the way that mail traveled. "That I have not the Propensity to sitting Still," he wrote ". . . let my present Journey witness for me, in which I have already travelled eleven hundred and forty Miles on this Continent [North America] since April and shall make Six hundred and forty Miles more before I see home."

Traveling by horse and carriage, Franklin surveyed roads used as postal routes and post offices in Virginia and toured New England, riding some 1,780 miles. He understood the importance of improving communication among the thirteen colonies. This was important for business, for

BENJAMIN FRANKLIN WAS POSTMASTER GENERAL FOR BOTH THE BRITISH GOVERNMENT IN COLONIAL TIMES AND THE EARLY AMERICAN GOVERNMENT. HE IMPROVED THE POSTAL SYSTEM'S SPEED AND EFFICIENCY. THIS ENGRAVING OF FRANKLIN WAS DONE BETWEEN 1763 AND 1785. HE LED THE POST OFFICE FOR MUCH OF THIS TIME.

exchanging political information, and for spreading the news. Franklin himself was a printer and publisher of the *Pennsylvania Gazette*. He made it easy and relatively inexpensive for newspapers to be sent through the mail. This happily increased his own profit.

But distances between the colonies were vast. Transportation was by horse, coach, or water, on poorly developed routes. Too often, riders and coaches delivering the mail had to travel on roads that were in terrible shape. They were "very bad, Incumbered with Rocks and mountainous passages, which were very disagreeable to my tired carcass," noted Sarah Kemble Knight, who kept one of the early descriptive journals of her eighteenth-century journey through Connecticut. Without a system of good roads and reliable carriers, delivery would not work smoothly, so Franklin personally inspected his territory.

MILESTONE 63 LIES ON THE BOSTON POST ROAD NEAR EAST BROOKFIELD, MASSACHUSETTS. MILESTONES WERE OFTEN CARVED OUT OF RED SANDSTONE BY LOCAL CRAFTSMEN. BENJAMIN FRANKLIN ENCOURAGED THEIR USE TO MARK THE ROUTES WHERE THE MAIL TRAVELED, BUT THERE IS NO EVIDENCE THAT HE ACTUALLY EVER PLACED ONE HIMSELF.

Then he set about making improvements. Milestones were set up alongside roads to mark the distance in miles to particular places to help guide riders. New routes were created to avoid difficult river crossings, which slowed travel. Franklin had riders on horseback carry the mail both day and night, speeding delivery time. By 1764, mail delivery—which until that time had taken about three weeks to travel from Philadelphia to Boston and back with a reply—now took six days. Colonial Americans went to a local post office to pick up their letters. In Philadelphia, Franklin established a "penny post": for an extra penny, people could receive their mail at home.

The colonial post even made a profit under Franklin—money that went to the British government. But that government was growing suspicious of his sympathies. Franklin clearly supported the movement for independence. The British dismissed him in 1774. The colonies, meeting in 1775 to form an American government, appointed Franklin the first postmaster general of what would become the United States.

Although during the Revolutionary War mail service was haphazard, communications that did get through contributed to America's success. Even before the Constitution was ratified in 1789, the new government recognized the value of a mail service. It established the "great post road" in 1785 to carry mail in stagecoaches from one end of the new country to the other: New Hampshire to Georgia. A post road established between Philadelphia and Pittsburgh extended the reach of the mail system west. The ratified Constitution included the congressional duty "to establish Post Offices and post Roads."

RIDERS ON HORSEBACK USUALLY CARRIED AND DELIVERED MAIL IN COLONIAL TIMES AND THE LATER PART OF THE EIGHTEENTH CENTURY. HERE, A LETTER IS HANDED OFF TO A WOMAN AT HOME. MAIL RIDERS FACED GREATER DANGER WHEN THEY CONVEYED MAIL TO MILITARY COMMANDERS DURING THE REVOLUTIONARY WAR.

Although some Founding Fathers, including Thomas Jefferson and James Madison, objected to a large, central federal government, they had little problem with a federal Post Office. They did not foresee that setting up a nationwide mail system could be contentious or controversial.

"The power of establishing post roads must, in every view, be a harmless power," wrote Madison, "and may, perhaps, by judicious management, become productive of great public conveniency." Madison thought, as many Americans after him did, that any system that encouraged communication among Americans could not "be deemed unworthy of the public care."

In 1792, President George Washington signed the first Post Office Act into law. It ensured that newspapers could continue to be sent relatively cheaply. In fact, newspapers and political reports and propaganda from congressmen dominated the mail. Sending personal letters was

PRESIDENT GEORGE WASHINGTON SIGNED THE FIRST POST OFFICE ACT INTO LAW IN 1792. HERE HE IS SHOWN ON ONE OF THE FIRST OFFICIAL STAMPS, PRINTED IN 1851. WASHINGTON APPEARS ON MORE AMERICAN STAMPS THAN ANY OTHER PERSON.

too expensive for most Americans. Since the British had routinely opened mail to spy on colonial Americans, the new law made it illegal to open another person's letter.

Before 1847, Americans had to pay for mail, but they did not use postage stamps to send a letter. A clerk at the post office marked the cost on the upper right corner of the envelope. The sender rarely paid this. The letter's receiver had to pay the cost or refuse to accept the mail. If he or she refused, the letter went back to the sender's post office. The postal system, although it had transported the letter both there and back, did not receive any payment.

Why would anyone refuse to accept a letter? In the first half of the nineteenth century, postage was expensive. The cost was based on how many sheets of paper were in the envelope and how far the letter needed to be transported. A one-page letter from New York City to Buffalo, New York, cost twenty-five cents to send in the 1840s. Many ordinary workers made just $1 a day or less. They were not going to spend so much on correspondence. Most letters, in fact, were sent by businesses.

Congress simplified postal rates in 1845. It authorized the first official printed stamps in 1847. Benjamin Franklin was pictured on the five-cent stamp, George Washington on the ten-cent stamp. Since then, Washington, followed by Franklin, has appeared on more U.S. stamps than any other subjects.

BENJAMIN FRANKLIN'S PORTRAIT IS SHOWN ON THIS ONE-CENT STAMP FROM 1851. LIKE GEORGE WASHINGTON, HIS IMAGE APPEARED ON ONE OF THE FIRST OFFICIAL STAMPS ISSUED IN 1847. FRANKLIN IS HONORED NOT ONLY FOR HIS ROLE AS POSTMASTER GENERAL BUT ALSO FOR HIS SERVICE AS A STATESMAN.

Americans did not rush to buy stamps: they were still not legally required. By 1852, less than 2 percent of United States mail carried postage stamps. In 1855, Congress passed a law that required all postage for mail to be paid with official stamps starting on January 1, 1856.

There were private mail services run by individuals and businesses, even in the eighteenth century, but the 1792 act banned them from carrying letters on established post roads. By 1800, the Post Office was transporting 2 million letters a year. This was a source of income it couldn't afford to lose. In 1823, Congress declared that waterways like rivers and lakes would be post roads. Railroads were declared post roads in 1838. This gave the advantage to the Post Office, as it limited how private postal services could move their mail.

WHO'S GOT MAIL?

STAGECOACHES TRANSPORTED MAIL FOR THE POST OFFICE THROUGHOUT THE NINETEENTH CENTURY. THIS COACH IS ON ITS WAY TO DEADWOOD CITY, SOUTH DAKOTA, IN 1889. STAGECOACHES CARRIED PASSENGERS AS WELL AS MAIL, BUILDING UP THE COUNTRY'S TRANSPORTATION SYSTEM.

Riders on horses or stagecoaches carried the mail on early routes. Into the nineteenth century, the Post Office continued to use riders and horses because they were cheaper and more reliably on time than any other method. This was especially true on routes that were less well traveled. Roads in Ohio, for example, were often carved out of dense forests that continued to loom over riders as they pressed their way through. Rivers were difficult to cross.

It took tough, fit people to deliver the mail through difficult terrain. "In the selection of riders you must always take persons of integrity, sound health, firmness, perseverance and high ambition, and pride of character," read one description of the job.

"Among these a preference is due to young men, the less the size the better."

But increasingly the Post Office relied on stagecoaches. As it would later do for the airplane industry, the Post Office helped to fund and expand the stagecoach business. Where stagecoaches traveled, the federal government improved roads. In addition to mail, coaches carried passengers, making it easier for the public to go west. Passengers gave an added advantage: if attacked by robbers, they could help the driver protect the mail. Carrying passengers also meant that the stagecoaches followed a regular schedule, although weather, muddy and icy roads, and the robbers just mentioned could affect delivery time.

Steamboats were also used to carry mail. Boat captains were informally carrying mail up and down the Mississippi River by 1812. So as not to lose business, the Post Office began contracting with steamboat owners in 1815. By the 1840s, the Post Office was issuing transportation contracts to single carriers, stagecoaches, and steamboats. In 1845, ever conscious of costs, Congress authorized the postmaster general to make sure the cheapest carrier for each route got the contract.

RIVERS WERE ALSO USED AS POSTAL ROUTES. STEAMSHIPS CARRIED MAIL AS EARLY AS THE 1810S. HERE, THE *MORNING STAR*, CONTRACTED BY THE POST OFFICE, TRANSPORTS U.S. MAIL ON THE OHIO RIVER IN 1858.

The 1845 law emphasized that it didn't matter what kind of transportation was used, as long as mail was delivered with "celerity [speed], certainty, and security." Those competing for contracts submitted what became known as "celerity, certainty, and security" bids. This was shortened to three asterisks—* * *—to stand for stars. These cheaper and usually more difficult and remote routes were nicknamed Star Routes.

HOW MANY WAYS CAN YOU TRANSPORT THE MAIL?

Over the years, Star Route carriers have used skis, flat-bottomed pole boats, mule trains, dogsleds, hovercraft, snowmobiles, and helicopters. In the late 1800s, Florida mail carriers would travel miles by sailboat and rowboat, then many more miles on foot across sandy beaches, between Palm Beach and Miami. Mail has been dropped by parachute in Alaska. Two-cylinder motorcycles began to be used in cities in 1914.

In the 1930s, Harry Elfers, who delivered mail from Sandusky, Ohio, to Kelleys Island in Lake Erie, used an "ironclad," or "flat-bottomed skiff," he explained. "There's a sail in the bow to carry us through the water or over the ice when conditions are right. There are two iron-shod runners on the bottom so the boat may be used as a sled. The sides are sheathed with galvanized iron. This is very important because thin ice will cut a boat like a knife."

The Post Office issued Star Route contracts to private carriers—often a single person—to carry the mail. Each carrier provided his or her own form of transportation. One early Star Route carrier in Wyoming traveled on horseback, then snowshoes, then a toboggan, to reach his destination. On one delivery, when his snowshoe broke, he managed to

Mail was delivered on Star Routes into the twentieth century. In 1970, the name "Star Route" was dropped in favor of "Highway Contract Routes," since motorized vehicles were the main form of transportation. But rural mail routes are still known popularly by the original name.

DOGSLEDS WERE USED TO CARRY MAIL IN THE NORTHERN UNITED STATES AND ALASKA INTO THE EARLY 1920S. THIS TEAM WAS PHOTOGRAPHED IN 1911. BECAUSE NEWSPAPERS AND PACKAGES WEIGHED MORE, DOGSLEDS USUALLY DID NOT CARRY THEM IN THE WINTER. WHEN SPRING CAME, THE PILED-UP MAIL WAS DELIVERED BY WAGON OR STEAMBOAT.

get back to his home, make another snowshoe, and attempt the delivery again. It took one week.

But overland Star Route carriers in the mid-nineteenth century could not deliver mail all the way from the eastern to the western United States. After gold was discovered in California in 1848, people flocked west to make their fortunes.

Steamboats were the first to carry mail there from the East Coast. They traveled south on the Atlantic Ocean until they arrived at the isthmus of Panama, a strip of land that connected North America to South America. Since construction did not begin on the Panama Canal until 1881 (it was completed in 1914), the mail crossed fifty miles of swamp and land by canoe and on pack animals. Then the mailbags were loaded onto another steamship when they reached the Pacific coast.

STEAMBOATS CARRIED MAIL FROM THE EAST COAST TO THE PACIFIC AFTER GOLD WAS DISCOVERED IN CALIFORNIA IN 1848. THEY ALSO MADE THE RETURN TRIP. HERE, A STEAMBOAT LEAVES THE HARBOR IN SAN FRANCISCO. THE BOATS GOING EACH WAY STOPPED IN PANAMA, WHERE THE MAIL WAS OFFLOADED AND TAKEN FIFTY MILES TO THE OTHER VESSEL.

CROSS-COUNTRY BY STAGE

Mail fared better than passengers on stagecoach rides. "I can remember no night of horror equal to my first night's travel on the Overland Route," wrote British naval lieutenant Edmund Hope Verney in 1865. He described his journey from San Francisco to New York:

"An American friend . . . had recommended me to bring an air-pillow [donut-shaped and filled with air]. This became my mainstay: I sat on it by day, or interposed it between the hard side of the coach and my ragged skin and jaded bones, and by night I put my head through the hole in the middle and wore it as a collar . . . This saved the sides of my head during my endeavours to sleep, but occasionally a heavier jolt than usual would strike my head violently against the roof, driving it [the pillow] down between my shoulders."

Verney mentioned his stop at a hotel in Virginia City, Nevada, where "more dead than alive I fell asleep on a real bed for several hours."

The sea routes steamships traveled to carry mail back and forth between the East and West Coast—including the trek over the Isthmus of Panama—often took more than the expected three to four weeks. When California was admitted as a state in 1850, it took six weeks for the news to reach

Los Angeles from Washington. The Post Office tried overland routes. From 1858 to 1861, the Butterfield Overland Mail transported mail by stagecoach from either Missouri or Tennessee to California in a little more than three weeks.

The most dramatic and celebrated way for mail to travel to California, however, was by the Pony Express. William Hepburn Russell, Alexander Majors, and William Bradford Waddell, experienced shippers of freight to the West, wanted a Post Office contract for a route from St. Joseph, Missouri, to Sacramento, California, and then by boat to San

GEORGE M. OTTINGER PAINTED THE ORIGINAL PICTURE OF A PONY EXPRESS RIDER, ENGRAVED IN 1867. HE RIDES THROUGH RUGGED TERRAIN, PASSING MEN STRINGING TELEGRAPH WIRES FROM POLE TO POLE. WHEN THE TRANSCONTINENTAL TELEGRAPH LINE WAS COMPLETED IN OCTOBER 1861, IT PUT THE PONY EXPRESS OUT OF BUSINESS.

Francisco. Although they started operating the Pony Express on April 3, 1860, they did not win an official contract until July 1, 1861.

In the meantime, they dazzled Americans with the swiftness of delivery and the daring of their riders. The Pony Express was set up as a relay in which one rider would travel at breakneck speed for about seventy-five to a hundred miles a day. He (there were no known women)

would change horses at stations that were ten to fifteen miles apart. Then the mail would be handed to the next rider, who continued on. The riders were often young: the average age was about twenty, and there were teenage riders perhaps as young as fourteen. They were small and lightweight, about the same size as a jockey racing horses today. They used special horses suited either to the flat terrain of the plains or to the treacherous terrain of the Rocky Mountains.

Although the public loved it, the Pony Express never made a profit. It was clearly faster than any other way to send the mail. It averaged ten days to cross the country. It famously delivered President Abraham Lincoln's 1861 inaugural address from Nebraska to California in seven days and seventeen hours. But the Pony Express was extremely expensive: at its beginning, it charged $5 ($130 today) to carry each half ounce of mail. Although later lowered to $1, the price was still too much for most people to pay. Riders mainly carried newspaper reports, business documents, and government communications.

On July 1, 1861, the U.S. Post Office finally began using the Pony Express to transport mail. Still, the express service continued to be in debt. When Western Union completed the last part of the transcontinental telegraph line at Salt

Lake City on October 24, 1861, there was a much faster way to send news from the East to the West. The Pony Express went out of business two days later, only nineteen months after it began.

HERE COMES THE PONY EXPRESS

Mark Twain described the excitement of seeing a Pony Express rider arrive at his destination:

> *"HERE HE COMES!"*
>
> *Every neck is stretched further, and every eye strained wider. Away across the endless dead level of the prairie a black speck appears against the sky, and it is plain that it moves . . .*
>
> *In a second or two it becomes a horse and rider, rising and falling, rising and falling . . . [A]nother instant a whoop and a hurrah from our upper deck, a wave of the rider's hand, but no reply, and man and horse burst past our excited faces, and go winging away like a belated fragment of a storm!*
>
> *So sudden is it all, and so like a flash of unreal fancy, that but for the flake of white foam left quivering and perishing on a mail-sack after the vision had flashed by and disappeared, we might have doubted whether we had seen any actual horse and man at all, maybe.*

2
SLAVERY, CIVIL WAR, AND THE MAIL

On July 29, 1835, a group of white men forced open a window at the Charleston, South Carolina, post office. Climbing in, they walked by mailbags full of ordinary letters to the shipment they were seeking: abolitionist newspapers and journals sent by the American Anti-Slavery Society in New York. The society had decided to use the mail system to spread the word in the South about the evils of slavery. It targeted ministers, politicians, and newspaper editors. Since it had few direct addresses, it sent the abolitionist literature in large batches to ministers and postmasters, hoping they would pass them on to their communities.

Instead, in Charleston, when word of the shipment got out, white residents demanded that the city's postmaster, Alfred Huger, turn the literature over to them. As a federal postmaster sworn to protect the mail, Huger would not; nor would he distribute the literature in the city. Instead, the shipment sat in the post office, where it was stolen in the break-in. The next night, an estimated 2,000 to 3,000 Charlestonians gathered to watch this "incendiary" mail burn. White southerners saw the mail campaign as a dangerous attack on their way of living, which was based on slavery. For the next week Huger collected all the mail from the steamships arriving from New York. Then he set aside the abolitionist literature in the post office.

ATTACK ON THE POST OFFICE, CHARLESTON, S.C.

THIS 1835 LITHOGRAPH SHOWS THE BREAK-IN AT THE CHARLESTON, SOUTH CAROLINA, POST OFFICE TO SEIZE ANTI-SLAVERY LITERATURE SENT FROM THE NORTH. ON THE LEFT, A CROWD BURNS THE MAIL, WHICH HAPPENED THE NEXT DAY. IT WAS TITLED "NEW METHOD OF ASSORTING THE MAIL, AS PRACTISED BY SOUTHERN SLAVE-HOLDERS." THE $20,000 REWARD SIGN IS THE BOUNTY PLACED ON THE HEAD OF ARTHUR TAPPAN, PRESIDENT OF THE AMERICAN ANTI-SLAVERY SOCIETY.

Although it was Huger's job to deliver the mail, not censor it, Postmaster General Amos Kendall backed his action. "We owe an obligation of the laws, but a higher one to the communities in which we live," said Kendall, "and if the *former* be perverted to destroy the *latter*, it is patriotism to disregard them." Kendall wrote to a postmaster in Louisiana that the postmasters in his state "will assuredly not be punished by me for obedience to the laws of their own state which forbids the circulation of seditionary [inciting to revolution] papers."

AMOS KENDALL WAS THE POSTMASTER GENERAL UNDER PRESIDENTS ANDREW JACKSON AND MARTIN VAN BUREN. HE SERVED FROM 1835 TO 1840. KENDALL SUPPORTED POSTMASTERS IN SLAVE-HOLDING STATES WHO KEPT ABOLITIONIST NEWSPAPERS AND PAMPHLETS THAT WERE MAILED TO THE SOUTH FROM REACHING THE PUBLIC.

President Andrew Jackson, who had appointed Kendall, called the mailing of abolitionist literature "a wicked plan of exciting the Negroes to insurrection and to massacre." Northern critics were enraged by this support for a federal official to censor the mail. In any case, the Anti-Slavery

Society soon abandoned the postal project because it was too complicated. Its action did nothing to decrease the rising tensions between the North and the South, which built over the next twenty-six years.

On April 12, 1861, the American Civil War between the Union (North) and the Confederacy (South) began. Even before the war started, several southern states came together at a provisional congress of the Confederate States. In February 1861, they formed their own Post Office and appointed its own postmaster general, John Henninger Reagan. Mail service from the North officially ended on May 31, 1861. The Confederate Post Office began operating on June 1.

LETTERS AND PACKAGES WERE VITAL TO THE MORALE OF BOTH UNION AND CONFEDERATE SOLDIERS DURING THE CIVIL WAR. HERE, DURING LEISURE TIME, UNION SOLDIERS OF THE MASSACHUSETTS LIGHT ARTILLERY, CAMPED IN MARYLAND, WRITE LETTERS HOME AS ONE SOLDIER SEWS HIS CLOTHING.

Both sides realized that letters from home could keep up morale in the military. Soldiers and their families needed to be connected by mail. Union soldier Newton Scott, away from his Iowa home for four years, wrote to his friend Hannah Cone, "Well, Miss Han, I will tell you that I . . . has written about a dozen letters since we left home, and received but two or three letters. This is the second one that I have written to you and received no answer." Miss Han did finally write to him with news of home. Being reminded of home helped soldiers to remember what they were fighting for.

"I know that a good cry does you good, and when I read your kind letter, I was about halfway between a laugh and a cry," John Cheney wrote from Mississippi to his wife. ". . . Sometimes I get a little blue, but, I just sit down and write to you, and it does me just as much good as it does you to cry."

PACKAGES FOR THE TROOPS

Families and friends did not only send letters to soldiers. "The mails during the war were very heavy and covered everything conceivable which came within the four pound limit," wrote a clerk in the Portland, Maine, post office; ". . . hats, caps, . . . shoes and all articles of clothing, watches, knives, pistols, etc.," were delivered. Boots were "sent singly to come within the law"—since one boot could weigh more than four pounds, they were sent one at a time.

"At Thanksgiving and Christmas, roast turkeys, chickens,

A large problem for exchanging mail with soldiers was that they kept moving from camp to camp and battle to battle. "We have moved so often that letters couldn't find us. Write often, and I will run the risk of getting the letters," wrote Union soldier Hermon Clarke to his father. To ensure that soldiers kept in touch as much as possible with their loved ones, the Union Army designated men specifically to collect and hand out the mail that arrived in camp. Tents and wagons became makeshift post offices.

The government knew that soldiers in the field had trouble getting stamps. Starting in July 1861, they could write "Soldier's Letters" on envelopes without stamps. Friends and

pies, puddings and other essentials to a holiday dinner were sent," continued the clerk. "And no doubt many a soldier['s] heart and stomach were made glad by a 'bite' from home."

THE POST OFFICE DID ITS BEST TO DELIVER MAIL TO SOLDIERS WHO WERE OFTEN ON THE MOVE. A U.S. MAIL VEHICLE BROUGHT LETTERS AND PACKAGES TO CAMPS, WHERE ARMY UNITS TOOK CARE OF FINAL DELIVERY. THIS WAGON, PHOTOGRAPHED IN 1864, TRANSPORTED MAIL FOR THE 2ND CORPS OF THE ARMY OF THE POTOMAC FIGHTING FOR THE UNION.

families paid the postage for Soldier's Letters upon receipt. By the end of 1864, the Post Office had started a system for the general public to send money orders. Soldiers and their families used this frequently to safely mail funds.

The Confederate Post Office drew on the expertise of southerners who had worked at the federal Post Office Department in Washington, DC. Many of them headed home to work for the Confederacy when the war started. By cutting costs and increasing postage rates, the Confederate Post Office was able to bring in some income in the early months. But with almost all the fighting taking place in the South, and with Union blockades of the Atlantic coastline limiting transport by sea, it became harder and harder to deliver the mail. The Confederacy also ran out of its own postage stamps. It could not use stamps issued by the U.S. government.

JOHN REAGAN RESIGNED FROM THE U.S. HOUSE OF REPRESENTATIVES WHEN HIS HOME STATE OF TEXAS SECEDED FROM THE UNION. HE WAS QUICKLY APPOINTED POSTMASTER GENERAL OF THE CONFEDERACY. REAGAN MADE A GREAT EFFORT TO KEEP THE CONFEDERATE POST OFFICE GOING, BUT THE WAR'S DESTRUCTION OF CONFEDERATE TERRITORY MADE IT INCREASINGLY DIFFICULT TO DELIVER MAIL.

In August 1861, the U.S. government prohibited mail from being sent between the Union and the Confederacy. It banned private carriers from delivering this mail as well. Any letters mailed to the South through the Post Office went to the Dead Letter Office. This was the office where letters whose addresses could not be read ended up. Letters to the Confederate States would not be delivered.

Prisoners of war on both sides received mail through a "flag of truce" system. The Union and the Confederacy named places where this mail—letters, small gifts, and sometimes food—could be exchanged along the border. Letters to and from prisoners of war were censored before they reached the exchange point. Civilians in southern cities and towns occupied by Union forces were also allowed to exchange letters under a "flag of truce."

Conditions in prisoner of war camps were very harsh on both sides and morale could be low. "For several months we suffered here very much for something to eat . . . ," wrote L. D. Hatch, a Confederate prisoner on Johnson's Island in Ohio. "The extreme cold of last winter . . . has been a severe shock to many of our men. I notice a great deal of sickness especially among the Prisoners captured at Nashville."

As the war progressed on the home front, U.S. Postmaster

General Montgomery Blair observed the long lines of people waiting to pick up mail at post offices in Washington, DC. Even in harsh weather they waited patiently for possible news from their loved ones. Mail only went from post office to post office. Recipients had to pick it up themselves or pay extra money—one or two cents—to the post office, or even more to a private carrier, for home delivery.

In 1863, Blair tried out a free home delivery service in forty-nine cities. Since home delivery required letter

MAIL SMUGGLERS IN HOOP SKIRTS

Government restrictions did not keep some letters from getting through to the opposite side. Individuals slipped past the border. In southern regions where the Union Army had taken over, such as New Orleans, Union commanders sometimes gave passes to relatives who wanted to visit family across the lines. Smugglers made runs across the boundaries of states bordering the Confederacy: Delaware, Kentucky, Maryland, Missouri, and West Virginia.

Women took an active part in smuggling. Many wore hoop skirts—skirts with a cage of steel bars underneath that held the fabric away from the body. Hoop skirts could shelter six

carriers to bring the mail from post offices to homes and businesses, it cost the Post Office money to hire more workers. In the first year, about 450 letter carriers were paid. Free home delivery was restricted to cities whose post offices would not go into debt because of this expense.

But more people began sending letters because it was easier. In 1864, the *Boston Daily* noted, "Everyone understands how great a convenience it is to be spared the necessity of going or sending to a distance . . . for a letter,

feet of space. They hid boots, clothing, food, and even weapons, as well as letters. In the first years of the war, officials were reluctant to stop women—and few wanted to search under their skirts. When a letter reached the destined side, the carrier dropped it in the right mailbox. As one friend called to a woman leaving Washington, DC, for Confederate Richmond, "Be sure and write quickly; you know how to get the letter through."

TWO WOMEN, CIRCA 1860, SHOW OFF THEIR FASHIONABLE HOOP SKIRTS. STEEL BARS HELD THE FABRIC AWAY FROM THE BODY TO CREATE SIX FEET OF SPACE UNDERNEATH. SINCE THE UNITED STATES FORBADE MAIL FROM TRAVELING TO THE CONFEDERACY, IT WAS OFTEN SMUGGLED ACROSS BORDERS, SOMETIMES UNDER THESE SKIRTS.

CITY HOME FREE DELIVERY STARTED DURING THE CIVIL WAR. BY 1900, THE POST OFFICE HAD HIRED MORE THAN 15,000 CARRIERS TO DELIVER MAIL. HERE, ONE POSES IN HIS UNIFORM, WITH MAILBAG, IN 1885. ONLY MEN CARRIED CITY MAIL UNTIL 1917, WHEN WORLD WAR I CAUSED A SHORTAGE OF MALE STAFF.

which may just as well be brought to his door." Free home delivery eventually paid for itself as Americans bought more stamps to mail their letters. By 1900, nearly eight hundred cities were on board, with more than 15,000 paid carriers.

When mail just went from post office to post office, letters did not require street addresses. There was no need, since recipients picked up the mail themselves. With home delivery, mail carriers did need to know exactly where to drop off letters and packages. Cities that wanted home delivery had to be sure that streets were named. Each house had to have an assigned number. Sidewalks and crosswalks were needed to make it easier for carriers to locate the right houses. This did not apply to rural routes. Americans living in the country had to wait another thirty years before mail would be delivered to their doors. Then their addresses were indicated by the number of the rural route they lived on.

The Civil War ended on April 9, 1865, and the U.S. Post Office worked to restore mail routes and service in the South. By November 1865, it had restored some 240 mail routes. By November 1866, a year later, it had regained control of a little more than a third of the post offices in the former Confederacy. The South could begin to take advantage of some of the changes to postal service the North had made during the war.

3

UPGRADING THE SYSTEM

RAILROAD MAIL, RURAL DELIVERY, AND PARCEL POST

Mail was generally sorted at the post office, but during the Civil War, in 1862, the head clerk at a Missouri post office tried a daring experiment. He placed clerks on the train between Hannibal and St. Joseph, who sorted and distributed the mail while the train was moving. They worked in a special car. It was fitted with a simple sorting table and a sorting case with pigeonholes for letters going to the different towns along the way. But Missouri was a border state with both Union and Confederate sympathizers living there. Continued violence between them brought an end to the experiment on that line in less than a year.

THE RAILWAY MAIL SERVICE RAN FROM 1864 TO 1977. CLERKS SORTED MAIL IN SPECIAL CARS LIKE THIS ONE, EQUIPPED WITH CUBBYHOLES TO SLOT THE LETTERS INTO FOR EACH TOWN ALONG THE LINE. THEY WERE THEN PLACED IN MAILBAGS TO BE DROPPED OFF AT THE RIGHT STATION.

In August 1864, the first official route of what became known as the Railway Mail Service began operating between Chicago and Clinton, Iowa. The plan was to save time by having mail sorted on the train and ready for delivery in towns along the way, instead of waiting for unsorted mail to arrive at

OWNEY THE POSTAL DOG

Owney, a terrier mix, began his life with the post office in Albany, New York, in 1888. He was likely owned by a mail clerk who left town. Owney stayed and the other clerks adopted him. He soon began riding in the wagons that carried mail from the post office to the train station. Then one day he rode on the railway mail car, which carried him from Albany to New York City and back. It was the first of nine years of travel on Post Office railcars. He eventually rode through forty-eight states.

In 1895, he joined a trip around the world, traveling with international deliveries of the mail. By then, the U.S. Post Office had agreements with postal services in other countries to continue delivery to a foreign address. Owney's trip lasted four months and took him by train to Canada and Mexico and by steamboat as far away as China and Japan.

The mail staff in Albany, afraid that Owney might get lost, got him a leather collar. The tag read: "Owney, Post Office, Albany, N.Y." Each time he traveled, railway mail clerks

the post offices. At each station, local postal workers picked up the sorted mail and delivered it within their communities.

Railway Mail Service continued to spread throughout the country, moving west and south. In 1898, a North Dakota newspaper reported that the oldest clerk in the Soo Line

fastened a baggage tag to his collar. These metal tags were weighing him down, so Postmaster General John Wanamaker had a little jacket made for him. When he wore the jacket, it helped distribute the weight of the metal.

Owney became the unofficial mascot of the Post Office. When he died in 1897, his body was preserved by taxidermy. He can now be visited at the National Postal Museum in Washington, DC.

OWNEY BECAME THE UNOFFICIAL MASCOT OF THE POST OFFICE IN THE LATE NINETEENTH CENTURY, AFTER HE STARTED RIDING ALONG WITH THE MAIL. THIS PHOTO, TAKEN IN 1895, SHOWS HIM WEARING HIS SPECIAL JACKET, CROWDED WITH BAGGAGE TAGS TO SHOW THE MANY PLACES TO WHICH HE TRAVELED.

"informs . . . [us] that eleven years ago . . . he took the first mail car out of St. Paul [Minnesota] . . . and on that occasion he had one package of about twenty letters on the car. Last Friday morning he left St. Paul on the same trip with 86 sacks of papers and 225 packages of letters. This is a remarkable increase in the postal business and is an evidence of the rapid development of this great northwest country."

By the end of the nineteenth century, more than 3,000 railroad clerks worked in nearly 2,000 mail cars. By 1930, more than 10,000 trains carried mail cars.

It wasn't easy to work as a railroad post office (RPO) clerk. Postmaster General John Wanamaker had said of all postal clerks, "On his memory, accuracy, and integrity hang the engagements of the business and social world. The postal service is no place for indifferent, sleepy or sluggish people." This was doubly true of those who sorted the mail as a train raced along. They had to have enormous memories to match a letter's destination to the best train route to take it there. Otherwise it would go into the wrong mailbag. They studied maps while taking breaks at stops along the route. They practiced with flash cards with the name of a city on one side and the best railroad route on the other.

RPO clerks also had to be strong. Mailbags weighed about two hundred pounds and they had to be lifted frequently. The clerk who had to drop off and pick up the mailbags at train stations had to be particularly strong. Some applicants did not make the cut because they got "seasick" working on a fast-moving train.

WORKING IN RAILROAD MAIL CARS COULD BE DANGEROUS SINCE TRAINS SOMETIMES CRASHED. THIS PHOTO SHOWS THE WRECK OF A TRAIN NEAR BEITNER, MICHIGAN, ON AUGUST 20, 1919. THE TRAIN COLLIDED HEAD-ON WITH ANOTHER ONE. A POSTAL CLERK WAS AMONG THOSE WHO DIED.

RPO clerks faced constant danger. The RPO cars were made of wood until the 1920s (when they began to be made from steel), and for decades they were lit by oil or gas lamps. They easily caught fire. Animals on the tracks, oncoming trains, broken rails, and washed-out bridges caused mail cars to derail. RPO clerks could be injured or killed in train wrecks. Between 1890 and 1905, 142 clerks lost their lives and hundreds more suffered serious injuries. Clerks were vulnerable to robbers, especially when mail cars carried millions of dollars. Cash or gold was sent by registered mail because it was cheaper for a business to pay the postage than to hire a private carrier.

Trains may have made the mail move faster, but it did not change the way all Americans received mail in their homes. Free home delivery started in 1863 for city dwellers, but thirty years later rural residents were still picking up their mail at the nearest post office. Yet in 1890 there were more people living in the country than in the city—some 41 million, about 65 percent of the population. They paid the same postage for sending mail as those in the city, for less service.

Postmaster General John Wanamaker proposed free delivery to rural homes in 1891. In 1896, Congress allowed

MAIL CRANES

An RPO clerk needed a way to be able to pick up and deliver bags of mail without having to stop the train. In 1867, L. F. Ward, a company in Ohio, invented a device called the "mail crane" to make the job easier. This was a wooden or sometimes metal scaffold fastened to the train platform. It held a mailbag at the height of the rail car. There were hooks at the top and bottom of the bag. A wooden "arm" stuck out so the bag would be close to the side of the mail car.

As the train passed by, a clerk on board used a metal bar to snag the bag. He pulled it into the car through an open doorway. At the same time, the clerk would push out the door a bag with mail for the town the train was passing through. It would fall to the ground for a later pickup by postal workers in the town. Sometimes the clerk would have to kick or throw the bag out. It wasn't easy to do while catching the waiting bag at the same time, but most clerks managed it.

RAILWAY MAIL CLERKS STOOD IN THE DOORWAYS OF THEIR TRAIN CARS TO DROP OFF OR PICK UP MAILBAGS AS THEY PASSED THROUGH A STATION. THESE CLERKS HAD TO BE QUICK AND STRONG TO DO THEIR JOB.

funding for a few routes in West Virginia. The experiment was very popular with rural Americans. By 1897, the Post Office had opened forty-four rural routes in twenty-nine states. The public clamored for more. Between 1896 and 1902, the Post Office received more than 10,000 petitions from rural communities requesting their own free delivery routes. The Rural Free Delivery (RFD) service was made permanent in 1902. Congress subsidized the cost.

By 1902, the Post Office had hired some 8,500 rural carriers. Some of them carried mail on the Star Routes. For most carriers it was a part-time job, as their main income was

RURAL FREE DELIVERY CARRIERS WERE CREATIVE IN USING VEHICLES THAT MET THE NEEDS OF THE AREA THEY COVERED. HERE, A RURAL CARRIER STANDS NEXT TO HIS 1926 MODEL T FORD, FITTED WITH SKIS TO GLIDE ACROSS NEW ENGLAND IN THE SNOW. IF THE WEATHER WAS GOOD, THE SKIS COULD BE RAISED AND WHEELS DROPPED INTO THEIR PLACE.

from farming. They often made their rounds in horse-drawn wagons and later in the first automobiles on the roads. In order to get their mail, rural citizens had to provide containers for letters to be left in. They used everything from pails to cigar boxes to syrup cans that might still be sticky.

RURAL FREE DELIVERY REQUIRED RECIPIENTS TO HAVE MAILBOXES, BUT THEY COULD BE IMPROVISED. TOP: ONE MAILBOX PERCHES ON AN OLD WAGON WHEEL IN MISSOURI IN THE 1930S. BOTTOM LEFT: A MAILBOX HANGS ON WIRES THAT USED A PULLEY TO BE HAULED ACROSS A CREEK IN VERMONT TO THE PLACE WHERE THE RESIDENTS LIVED. BOTTOM RIGHT: A MAILBOX SITS ATOP A GAS PUMP IN ALABAMA.

Eventually, manufacturers began making standardized mailboxes, guided by the Post Office's recommendations: to be made of metal, waterproof, and able to be fastened to a post at a height that the carrier would be able to reach in from a car with "one gloved hand in the severest weather."

One woman in Colorado expressed her thanks for having "our mail [delivered] fresh instead of stale." "I am more than

COMMEMORATING HISTORY THROUGH STAMPS

The 1890s were an innovative time for the Post Office. Stamp collecting became popular in the 1860s, but not until 1893 did the Post Office issue its first "commemorative" stamp. These stamps honored an important or popular person, event, organization, or cultural trend in American history. They were sold for only a limited period of time, and collectors were eager to buy them. The first commemorative marked the 1893 World's Columbian Exposition, a world's fair in Chicago.

Commemorative stamps can be any shape and size. The Columbian stamps were twice the size of regular stamps. The first triangular stamp was made in 1997; the first round stamp appeared in 2000. In 2017, the U.S. Postal Service issued a "Total Eclipse of the Sun" stamp. The stamp appeared to be a black dot. But because it was made with heat-sensitive ink,

ever proud of being an American citizen," wrote a country dweller in Arizona to the Post Office. ". . . I live three and a half miles from the Tempe post-office, and have been sick for a week past, yet my mail is brought to my door every morning, except Sunday."

As RFD spread across the country, the roads leading to farms and villages were improved by the government,

when touched, it showed an image of the moon. In 2018, "Frozen Treats" stamps were scratch-and-sniff. By scratching the image, a person could smell an ice-cream pop or a Popsicle in different flavors.

In 1993, USPS issued its most popular and bestselling stamp to date, of the singer Elvis Presley, who died in 1977. More than 500 million Elvis stamps have been printed. Their face value is twenty-nine cents. Because there are so many, though, collectors can buy them for a few cents today—but they are still worth twenty-nine cents each if used as postage.

THE FIRST COMMEMORATIVE STAMPS WERE ISSUED IN 1893. THIS 3-CENT STAMP, ISSUED IN 1940, COMMEMORATES THE "75TH ANNIVERSARY OF THE 13TH AMENDMENT TO THE CONSTITUTION." THE AMENDMENT, WHICH ENDED SLAVERY, WENT INTO EFFECT IN 1865.

making transportation easier in general. In addition, rural delivery "had become a great university in which 36,000,000 of our people receive their daily lessons from the newspapers and magazines of the country," wrote South Carolina congressman A. F. Lever in 1906. "It is the schoolhouse of the American farmer, and is without doubt one of the most potent educational factors of the time."

RFD BROUGHT NEWS AND INFORMATION AS WELL AS PERSONAL LETTERS AND PACKAGES TO RURAL COMMUNITIES. HERE, TWO CHILDREN IN THE MISSOURI OZARKS RETRIEVE A NEWSPAPER FROM THE FAMILY MAILBOX IN 1940. SPREADING THE NEWS TO EVERY PART OF AMERICA WAS ONE OF POSTMASTER GENERAL BENJAMIN FRANKLIN'S MAIN GOALS DURING THE YEARS LEADING UP TO THE REVOLUTIONARY WAR.

RFD mail carriers often understood that their service was community building. They were usually happy to do anything to help their neighbors. "We have . . . given first-aid treatment . . . have had to help in sickness and death," explained a rural carrier from Virginia in 1936. "We have extracted livestock from fences and called the veterinarian in emergency cases . . . One time I had to carry a tiny baby from its sick mother to where the old grandma lived several miles away. We cannot class such things as duties. They are all blessed privileges. Our patrons are not just patrons, they are more than that. They are our friends."

Spread out across the country, Americans needed the Post Office to deliver items that were hard to get in local shops. By the end of the nineteenth century, mail order business was booming. People could order household items, clothes, farm implements, furniture, and even steam engines from catalogs. The goods available without leaving one's home seemed endless, like those offered by the internet today.

Mail order businesses sent the items people ordered through the mail. But before 1913, the Post Office only carried packages that weighed no more than four pounds. Private delivery firms transported the rest, charging large fees.

These private companies also did not reach every part of the country, particularly where travel was difficult. Since rural Americans depended on shipments for everything from tools to food to winter coats to medicines, they were eager to have the Post Office handle the delivery. As *Harper's* magazine had pointed out in 1889, "Express companies extend their business wherever it promises to pay. The Post-office extends its operations wherever there are settlers."

POSTAL WORKERS LIKE THESE IN PIE TOWN, NEW MEXICO, IN 1940, HELPED BUILD
AND TIE TOGETHER COMMUNITIES. THEY NOT ONLY DELIVERED MAIL BUT ALSO
PROVIDED HELP, AND SOMETIMES MEDICAL CARE, TO RURAL AMERICANS LIVING
FAR APART FROM ONE ANOTHER.

MAIL ORDER TAKES OFF

Two businesses dominated the early mail order market. Montgomery Ward opened in Chicago in 1872. Founder Aaron Montgomery Ward originally listed 163 items for sale, printed on a single sheet of paper. Soon a catalog cover proclaimed that Montgomery Ward carried "Supplies for Every Trade and Calling on Earth." Sears, Roebuck & Company began in Chicago in 1893.

THESE PAGES FROM THE 1902 SEARS CATALOG SHOW SOME OF THE MANY TOYS THAT COULD BE ORDERED. THIS PAGE FEATURES "OTHER ACTION TOYS OF QUALITY." THE POST OFFICE WOULD DELIVER ONE STRAIGHT TO YOUR DOOR.

Congress finally responded by passing a parcel post act in 1912. Parcel post was a huge success. In the first five days alone, 4 million packages passed through the Post Office. In the first six months, 300 million packages were mailed. The service was a great boost to the economy.

From its beginning, creative Americans used parcel post to ship their goods. On January 26, 1913, the *New York*

At first it sold gold watches by mail. In 1896, it produced its first general catalog. In 1900 it advertised itself as the "cheapest supply house on earth." In a 1903 article in the *Atlanta Constitution*, Sears declared that "one-fourth of the entire population of the United States secures some of their goods from the Chicago Mail Order Houses," which included competitor Montgomery Ward. There was more than enough business for both of them.

The items one could buy by mail included medical and veterinary supplies, musical instruments, bicycles, sewing machines, and baby carriages. Sears began selling "house kits" in 1908, so people could construct homes to live in. There were 447 models, ranging in price from about $750 to nearly $6,000. The company promised that "we will furnish all the material to build this [house]." The parts arrived ready to assemble. The special Christmas catalogs offered Mickey Mouse watches, train sets, and live canaries, among other things.

Times reported: "John Oswald, a manufacturer of ice cream, to-day by parcel post, sent a quart can of ice cream from [Nyack, New York] to another town of Rockland County. Mr. Oswald has invented a box made of pressed cork in which cream can be kept frozen for seven hours without being packed in ice. The parcel post will be used as a means of conveyance for ice cream in this country hereafter."

Since people would mail almost anything—including children—the Post Office soon issued rules for what could not be mailed. These items included indecent or immoral articles, alcoholic beverages, and "live or dead (and not stuffed) animals, birds, or poultry." But sending bees and bugs was allowed, and beginning in 1918, day-old chicks

KIDS BY MAIL

The baby son of Mr. and Mrs. Jesse Beagle of Ohio appears to be the first child sent by parcel post—to avoid the high cost of passenger train tickets—in January 1913. The *New York Times* reported that he was safely delivered to his grandmother. In 1913 and 1914, other newspapers occasionally reported the shipping of children through the mail. The *Fairmont West Virginian* on January 12, 1914, chronicled the story of a mother in Lebanon, Ohio. She told the local postmaster that she wanted to send her baby to the child's grandmother. "The babe was weighed, stamped and a tag tied around its neck," the newspaper said.

The *Bryan (Texas) Daily Eagle and Pilot* picked up an Associated Press story on February 3, 1914: "Mrs. E. H. Staley today received by parcel post her two-year-old nephew, who had been visiting his grandmother at Stratford, Okla. The postage was 18 cents and the boy arrived in good condition."

could be sent. By then, letters and packages had a revolutionary new way to travel.

PARCEL POST ALLOWED FARMERS TO SEND EGGS DIRECTLY TO THEIR CUSTOMERS IN CITIES. THIS METAL CONTAINER, USED SOMETIME BETWEEN 1916 AND 1920, HELD SEVENTY-TWO FRESH EGGS.

The *New York Times* of February 4 recorded that the nephew "was transported 25 miles by rural route before reaching the railroad. He rode with the mail clerks [and] shared his lunch with them."

Perhaps the best-known child-by-mail story is that of Charlotte May Pierstorff of Idaho. Rather than buy an expensive train ticket, her parents sent five-year-old Charlotte by parcel post to her grandmother's house, about seventy-three miles away. It cost fifty-three cents. Charlotte's mother's cousin, who was a railway mail clerk, chaperoned the girl. It is said that because of this trip, Postmaster General Albert S. Burleson finally forbade the mailing of children later in 1914.

CHARLOTTE MAY PIERSTORFF WAS MAILED BY PARCEL POST TO HER GRANDMOTHER'S HOUSE. THE FEW CHILDREN KNOWN TO HAVE BEEN MAILED WERE OFTEN ENTRUSTED TO RELATIVES WHO WORKED ON THE MAIL TRAINS IN WHICH THEY TRAVELED.

4

MAIL MOVES
UP INTO THE AIR AND OUT INTO THE SUBURBS

Almost 5,000 people stood in a large field outside of Washington, DC, on May 15, 1918. The crowd included kids who had been given the day off from school; Alexander Graham Bell, the inventor of the telephone; future president Franklin D. Roosevelt; and President Woodrow Wilson and his wife, Edith. They had all come to see one of the first two airplanes officially carrying the United States mail take off.

The pilot that day was Lieutenant George Leroy Boyle, who was provided by the U.S. Army. Since commercial

LIEUTENANT GEORGE BOYLE (*RIGHT*) AND MAJOR REUBEN FLEET STAND NEXT TO THE AIRPLANE BOYLE WOULD FLY TO PHILADELPHIA ON ITS WAY TO NEW YORK, ON MAY 15, 1918. THIS WAS THE LAUNCH OF THE U.S. POST OFFICE'S AIRMAIL SERVICE, BUT BOYLE DID NOT MAKE IT TO HIS DESTINATION BECAUSE HE TRAVELED IN THE WRONG DIRECTION.

flying had not developed, most pilots got their experience flying military planes. His plane could fly only some 175 miles before it needed to refuel. Boyle would land in Philadelphia, where another Army pilot would take over, completing the route to Hempstead, a town near New York City. At the same time Boyle left Washington, another pilot would take off from Hempstead on his way to Philadelphia. A fourth pilot would finish the last leg to Washington.

With the mail already on board, Boyle climbed into his cockpit. The plane's engine wouldn't start. It did not have any fuel. The ground crew quickly filled the tank. Finally, the plane took off. In 1918 there were few markers to guide a pilot. Boyle thought he was following the railroad tracks north to Philadelphia, but he wasn't. He flew south instead and landed in a field in Maryland. His plane turned over and the propeller broke. The mail he carried had to be taken to New York by train. The pilot earned the nickname "Wrong Way Boyle." Luckily, the mail that left New York for Washington did make it all the way by plane.

This was not a perfect beginning for the U.S. Post Office Airmail Service. But the airplanes that early pilots flew were not like the ones today. The first airplane flight had happened only fifteen years earlier, on December 17, 1903, when Orville and Wilbur Wright made four test runs; the longest they stayed in the air that day was 59 seconds, and the plane flew only 852 feet.

EARLY AIRPLANES WERE FLIMSY AND COULD BE DANGEROUS TO FLY—AND EVEN MORE DANGEROUS IF THEY CRASHED. THIS 1918 PHOTO SHOWS ARMY PILOT LT. WEBB CLIMBING UP THE UNDERSIDE OF HIS WRECKED AIRMAIL PLANE. THE U.S. AIRMAIL SERVICE ENDURED DESPITE THESE CHALLENGES.

In 1918, planes were made of cloth stretched over wood, and the pilot sat open to the air. An article in the *Air Service Journal,* "Practical Hints on Flying," suggested to pilots that they "never forget that the engine may stop, and at all times keep this in mind." They had no reliable instruments or radios to guide them and no lights at the places they landed. They could not fly at night.

By August, the Post Office had taken over the airmail service so it would work more efficiently. It hired civilian pilots. It also purchased six planes built especially to carry the mail. Routes were added and extended. By 1920, they stretched from New York to Reno, Nevada, on the way to San Francisco.

Planes flew in the daylight. At night the mail was transported by train. When daylight dawned again, it was put on another plane. The first delivery all the way to San Francisco, with the pilots flying both day and night, was in February 1921.

On February 22, two planes took off from New York and two from San Francisco. Each was crossing the country to deliver the mail to the opposite city. One of the pilots heading east crashed and died in Nevada. His mail was flown to a town in Nebraska. There, pilot James H. "Jack" Knight, who had been an Army flight instructor, took over the delivery. He headed for Omaha—at night. It was the first time he had flown in the dark. The towns he passed over lit bonfires to help him find his way. "I felt I had a thousand friends on the ground—Lexington, Grand Island, Columbus, Fremont slipped by, warm glows of well-wishers beneath the plane's wings," Knight later remembered.

In Omaha, Knight discovered that there was no pilot to continue on to Chicago. He took on the job. When he arrived at the landing field in Iowa City to refuel, there were no lights. Everyone had gone home, thinking the flight had been canceled. He "buzzed" the field, flying low and fast to make a buzzing sound. The night watchman heard the sound. He set out railroad flares so Knight could see the field. After landing and refueling, he continued on to Chicago. "I was flying over territory that was absolutely strange," Knight recalled. "I knew nothing of the land markings, even if they had been visible. I had to fly by compass and by feel." He landed the next morning in Chicago. Other planes finished the trip to New York.

IN 1921, PILOT JACK KNIGHT TOOK OVER FOR A DOWNED PILOT IN NEVADA TO FLY THE DIFFICULT LEG FROM NEBRASKA TO CHICAGO. HIS FLIGHT WAS PART OF THE POST OFFICE'S EFFORT TO QUICKLY TRANSPORT THE MAIL FROM SAN FRANCISCO TO NEW YORK. THE ENTIRE FLIGHT, WITH KNIGHT'S HELP, SET A RECORD FOR SPEED. AN IMPRESSED CONGRESS INCREASED FUNDING FOR THE AIRMAIL PROGRAM.

This mail run from San Francisco to New York took 33 hours and 20 minutes. It was a record time. It would not have happened without Knight. Several pilots had made the trip, but newspapers singled him out as a hero, "the guy who saved the night mail." Before this flight, Congress had been ready to cut funds for the program. After this, it increased them.

If the Post Office were to continue airmail, though, it had to make some improvements. Airplanes were fitted with instruments that glowed in the dark, lights to

navigate, and parachute flares. In 1923, the Post Office began lighting the routes along the ground. The first lighted section was between Chicago and Cheyenne, Wyoming, a treacherous passage. There, the Post Office installed emergency landing fields every twenty-five miles. These fields had fifty-foot towers with lights that revolved so pilots could see them from a distance. They could spot beacons on the main airfields from up to

THIS 1921 PHOTO SHOWS THE AIRMAIL PLANE HANGAR AT THE IOWA CITY, IOWA, AIRFIELD. TOWERS TO HELP GUIDE PILOTS STAND BESIDE IT. IOWA CITY WAS ONE OF THE STOPS ON THE POSTAL SERVICE'S TRANSCONTINENTAL ROUTE FROM NEW YORK CITY TO RENO, NEVADA. BUILT IN 1918, IT IS THE OLDEST CIVIL AIRPORT WEST OF THE MISSISSIPPI RIVER STILL OPERATING IN ITS ORIGINAL LOCATION.

"FATHER OF THE AIR MAIL"

Clyde Kelly, a congressman from Pennsylvania, became known as the "father of the air mail." He worked to ensure that the experiment with airmail—and the young air transport industry—would not be abandoned before it was solidly established. Kelly was assigned to the House Committee on Post Office and Post Roads. He sponsored the Air Mail Act of 1925 (known as the Kelly Act). This gave the Post Office the ability to contract with commercial airlines to carry the mail.

Kelly saw the postal system as a work in progress, always trying to improve. "The great postal highway of the United States is the people's thoroughfare," he said in 1931. "It was not built in a day or a generation, nor is its task finished today, but its record in the past is the inspiring promise of its betterment in the future."

150 miles away. These improvements were made on other routes. By 1925, lighted airways for mail flights reached from New York to Salt Lake City.

The Post Office found hiring its own pilots and using its own planes were not cost-effective and did not deliver mail quickly enough. The Air Mail Act of 1925 gave the Post Office the ability to offer contracts to private aircraft companies for airmail service. By 1926, nearly all these contract routes were operating. Charles Lindbergh flew the route between Chicago and St. Louis. In 1927, Lindbergh became famous by setting the record for flying solo across the Atlantic Ocean, from the United States to France. The early contractors included the companies that would become Trans World Airlines (TWA), American Airways, United Airlines, and Eastern Air Lines.

In these early years—the 1920s and the 1930s—few passengers flew on airplanes. It was Post Office funding for carrying the

PILOT CHARLES LINDBERGH IS SHOWN HERE IN 1923 IN AN OPEN COCKPIT AIRPLANE IN ST. LOUIS, MISSOURI. IN 1926, HE FLEW THE MAIL UNDER CONTRACT WITH THE POST OFFICE FOR THE ROBERTSON AIRCRAFT CORPORATION. HIS ROUTE WENT BETWEEN ST. LOUIS AND CHICAGO.

mail that kept the fledgling commercial airlines in business. Its support was especially important after the stock market crash in October 1929, which started the Great Depression.

In 1924, the first U.S. mail was delivered by plane from Fairbanks to McGrath, Alaska, a distance of 280 miles. Pan

American Airways, contracted by the U.S. Post Office, flew the first airmail from the mainland to Hawaii in 1935. In addition to servicing these territories, in 1927 the Post Office began regularly scheduled international airmail delivery. The first route went from Key West, Florida, to Havana, Cuba. Flights across the Pacific Ocean began in 1935 and across the Atlantic to Europe in 1939. Airmail service to Africa was launched in 1941. Not only were Americans quickly connected to each other; they began to be connected to the world.

Both planes and ships transported mail overseas during World War II (1941–1945). The war brought a flood of letters to the Post Office. With soldiers, sailors, marines, airmen, and coastguardsmen stationed in Europe and in the Pacific, distances were long. Bags of letters took up valuable space. The space was needed for carrying military supplies and equipment. The government came up with "Victory Mail"— V-mail—a way to use special paper and microfilm to make letters less bulky. "An air-mail sack weighs about 70 pounds. By the use of V-mail forms . . . the same 70 pounds can be reduced to two pounds," explained Frank Walker, the post-master general at the time.

The Post Office was responsible for collecting all mail,

both regular letters and V-mail. It separated out the V-mail and sent it on to either the Army or Navy post offices. A V-mail letter was written on an 8-and-a-half-by-11-inch piece of thin writing paper. This was available for free from the Post Office. It could only be used by family and friends sending letters to the military. American civilians wrote and sent their mail the usual way, on ordinary paper through regular post offices.

The area for writing the body of the letter as well as the mailing address and the return address of the sender were part of the same piece of V-mail paper. There was no envelope; instead the letter was folded and sealed. Once the letter was sent, it was photographed onto 16mm microfilm. Some 1,500 to 1,800 V-mail letters fit on a ninety-foot roll of film. A roll of film weighed 4 ounces. With this process, about 150,000 "letters" could fit into

V-MAIL WRITING PAPER AND ENVELOPE CAME AS ONE SHEET. HERE, THE ADDRESS SIDE SHOWS INSTRUCTIONS FOR HOW TO USE THE SYSTEM. CORRESPONDENTS WROTE THEIR LETTERS ON THE OTHER SIDE, THEN FOLDED AND SEALED THE SINGLE PIECE OF PAPER.

a single forty-five-pound mailbag, instead of the thirty-seven mailbags ordinary letters would have required.

When a letter arrived at its destination, each frame of the film was printed onto a sheet of paper. The paper was cut into individual letters, which were folded and sent on to the recipients. Mail to soldiers and mail back to the home front were processed the same way. They were one-quarter of the size of the original letter. If the ink used was not dark enough or the handwriting too small, they were very hard to read.

THIS POST OFFICE ANNOUNCEMENT PROMOTING THE USE OF V-MAIL ENCOURAGED AMERICANS TO "SPEED YOUR LETTERS TO OUR ARMED FORCES OVERSEAS BY MICRO-FILM PHOTO-GRAPH." OFFICIAL V-MAIL LETTER SHEETS WERE AVAILABLE FOR FREE TO CIVILIANS, WHO COULD PICK UP TWO SHEETS A DAY FROM THEIR LOCAL POST OFFICE, AND MILITARY PERSONNEL, WHO OBTAINED THEM WHERE THEY WERE STATIONED.

Between June 1942 and November 1945, the system delivered more than a billion V-mail letters. By 1944, it had saved space for almost 5 million pounds of military supplies and equipment heading overseas.

Another problem during World War II was the increased volume of mail. There were so many more letters and packages moving through the system that it swamped postal workers trying to sort it. Many American men and some women had gone off to war. Substitute postal workers did not have the knowledge or memory to quickly identify and sort by individual addresses in thousands of locations. In 1943, the Post Office began adding one or two numbers between the city and state for mail going to large cities. For example, the new address would read "Minneapolis 16 Minnesota." These numbers indicated which zone or area within the city an address was located. Workers could pre-sort by zone before they sorted by individual addresses. This was the forerunner of the zip code system established in the early 1960s.

After World War II, the Post Office was busier than ever. Between 1940 and 1960, the volume of mail went from about 28 billion to a little less than 64 billion pieces a year. In the postwar economic boom, more and more houses were built, adding many new addresses to the postal system. Americans were moving out from the city to the suburbs. The growth of suburbs required new, spread-out delivery routes. The Post Office began providing mail carriers with motorized vehicles beginning in 1950. These included the Mailster, a three-wheeled mini-truck; by 1966, nearly 18,000 of them were in use across the country. Many rural carriers, however, continued to use their own vehicles for delivering the mail.

MAIL FOR THE INTERNED

Mail was a lifeline for all prisoners of war held by enemy forces. It also became one for those Japanese Americans held in internment camps in the United States. These camps were set up to house both people born in Japan and those born in the United States to Japanese parents. The government wrongly feared that during World War II they would be loyal to Japan, not to America.

Taken from their homes—mainly on the West Coast—and forced to live in desolate locations, interned Japanese Americans appreciated words from the outside. "After hearing that the afternoon mail came in, I hurried to the post office. Yes, as usual the line was a block long and that meant I was at the end of the line and oh what a long wait that was," wrote Louise Ogawa to Clara Breed in April 1942. Breed was a white librarian who sent care packages to the Japanese American teenagers she had known in San Diego. "I was told that I had a package awaiting me . . . to my surprise it was a book. And I was so happy I felt like shouting."

At first white postal clerks were brought in from surrounding towns to run the camp post offices. "They did not know one Japanese name from another and we had to stand in line for hours before we could get our mail," remembered Tetsuzo Hirasaki. But several Japanese Americans had worked for the Post Office before they were interned. The Post Office finally put them on the job and mail day went more smoothly.

In 1988, the U.S. government formally apologized for interning Japanese-born and American-born Japanese Americans. Those who were still alive received reparations—a small payment of money—for what they had suffered.

THE POST OFFICE AT THE INTERNMENT CAMP FOR JAPANESE AMERICANS OUTSIDE DENSON, ARKANSAS, IN 1942. THE LOCAL WHITE POSTMASTER, FRED R. PARIS, EXPLAINS PROCEDURES TO THE CAMP'S RESIDENTS, WHO HELP SORT OUTGOING MAIL.

At the same time, fewer and fewer Americans were riding on trains. They preferred using their own cars. As there were fewer trains, the use of railroads to transport mail declined. A system of Highway Post Offices was created: buses on which postal clerks sorted mail between stops, as they had on trains. The last Post Office bus traveled between Cincinnati and Cleveland, Ohio, in 1974.

A FLEET OF MAILSTERS APPEARS IN A HOLIDAY PARADE, CIRCA 1954, TO SHOWCASE THE POST OFFICE'S NEWEST VEHICLE. MAILSTERS WERE THREE-WHEELED, GAS-POWERED MINI-TRUCKS USED BY LETTER CARRIERS STARTING IN THE MID-1950S. EACH COULD HOLD SOME FIVE HUNDRED POUNDS OF MAIL AS WELL AS A DRIVER.

Many of the older city post offices had been built near railway stations. They were not conveniently located to take in and dispatch the larger volume of mail or accommodate the trucks and airplanes now used to carry mail. New facilities and new routes had to be created. But improving transportation methods was only one of the problems the Post Office faced when the 1960s began.

5

FROM POST OFFICE DEPARTMENT TO UNITED STATES POSTAL SERVICE

The Chicago Post Office, completed in 1934, was the largest post office building in the world. It covered more than 2 million square feet of floor space. It could process 35 million letters, as well as 500,000 mailbags full of newspapers and parcels, every day. Each day 125 trains carried mail to and from a station underneath the building. Its lobby, in the art deco style, was lavish, with marble and gold glass mosaic tiles.

But in October 1966, processing the mail there came to a jarring halt. By then, most mail was carried in trucks, not

THE INTERIOR OF THE CHICAGO POST OFFICE, HERE PHOTOGRAPHED IN 1964, WAS RICHLY DECORATED, AN IMPRESSIVE VISUAL SYMBOL OF THE GREATNESS OF THE UNITED STATES AND ITS GOVERNMENT. BUT THE BUILDING COULD NOT HANDLE THE ENORMOUS FLOW OF MAIL PASSING THROUGH IT. OVERLOADED, IT SHUT DOWN FOR TEN DAYS IN 1966.

on trains. There was not enough room for these trucks to dock and unload. They stretched in long lines around the post office. Trains stuffed with mailbags remained under the building. Mail volume had increased dramatically since 1934, but the number of regular postal workers had not. "About 1,000 volunteer postal workers toiled today to clear a backlog of a million pieces of mail at the main post office [in Chicago]," the *New York Times* reported on October 10. The backlog got worse.

"At the peak of the crisis in Chicago, ten million pieces of mail were logjammed. The sorting room floors were bursting with more than 5 million letters, parcels, circulars, and magazines that could not be processed," Postmaster General Lawrence F. O'Brien later explained to Congress. "Outbound mail sacks formed small grey mountain ranges while they waited to be shipped out.

"Our new and beleaguered Chicago postmaster . . . summed it up pretty well when he said: 'We had mail coming out of our ears.'"

Postal officials were forced to close the Chicago post office for ten days to clear the jam. Mail went to Nashville, Milwaukee, and Kansas City to be sorted. This caused crunches in these cities. At one point the Post Office considered burning piles of undelivered marketing mail—advertising flyers sent to every address in the city. The companies that had mailed them protested. Even so, the flyers were delivered weeks after the sale prices they offered had expired.

The Post Office and Congress worried that the Chicago crisis would happen again, there or in other places. Although the Post Office was relying more and more on trucks and airplanes, the older buildings were not set up to handle deliveries from these vehicles. Not only the buildings but the equipment inside was often out of date.

POSTAL WORKERS SORT MAIL IN 1966, IN A FACILITY NEAR WASHINGTON, DC. BETWEEN 1945 AND 1970, THE NUMBER OF PIECES OF MAIL HANDLED BY THE POST OFFICE INCREASED BY 224 PERCENT. POSTAL OFFICIALS FEARED THAT OUTDATED BUILDINGS AND EQUIPMENT COULD NOT MANAGE THE LOAD.

Besides this, the amount of mail a post office handled had grown dramatically. In 1945, nearly 38 billion pieces of mail passed through post offices. By 1970, mail volume had increased to nearly 85 billion pieces. "We are trying to move our mail through facilities largely unchanged since

INTRODUCING MR. ZIP

To help speed up the process of delivering the mail, on July 1, 1963, the Post Office introduced zip codes. "Zip" stood for "Zoning Improvement Program." Each address in the United States was given a five-digit zip code. This code meant that mail could quickly be sent to regional sorting stations. It could then be sorted by street number address.

Zip codes do not correspond to each state. States usually contain complete zip code areas, but some zip codes cross state borders. The first digit indicates which broad geographical area of the United States an address is located in. These numbers range from 0 for the Northeast to 9 for the far West. The next two digits indicate a large city post office or sectional center located near major transportation networks. The last two digits indicate small post offices or the delivery area.

The first zip code ever issued was 00602, given to a large part of Puerto Rico, a territory of the United States.

the days ... when our mail volume was 30 percent of what it is today," Postmaster General O'Brien told Congress.

Congress was also concerned about costs and profit. Increased mail volume brought in more money. But it was not enough to offset the expense of processing and delivering

Puerto Rico was the farthest east moving from right to left across the country. The Internal Revenue Service (IRS) now has an even lower zip code: 00501. This zip code includes only the IRS offices in Holtsville, New York. The highest zip code—99950—covers Ketchikan, Alaska. For individual people, only the president of the United States and the First Lady or Gentleman have their own zip codes: 20500-0001 and 20500-0002.

Businesses were very happy with the zip code system. It allowed them to easily target entire neighborhoods for advertising. They translate well into bar codes. Private mail companies use the postal system zip codes too.

An additional four digits were added to the end of the five-digit zip code in 1983. They more accurately pinpoint the location of an address. Although USPS does not require the extra four digits, it does require the five-digit zip code on any item mailed.

the mail. When a company spends more money than it earns, it builds up a deficit. By the late 1960s, the Post Office had a deficit of more than $1 billion.

On March 18, 1970, letter carriers in New York City started a wildcat strike. A wildcat strike is one that is not approved by the official union, in this case the National Association of Letter Carriers. Federal workers were banned from striking. But the letter carriers said they were underpaid. "The reason we went on strike," remembered letter carrier Frank Orapello, "is because we just couldn't live in New York City with the amount of money we made as a postal employee. Everybody had two or three jobs."

Postal workers had heard that Congress was considering giving them a pay raise of 4 to 5.4 percent of their salary. They also knew that, the year before, Congress had given its members a raise of 41 percent. Within a week after the March 18 strike was called, the New York letter carriers had been joined by postal workers in more than thirty cities. The strikers included clerks and mail handlers as well as carriers. An estimated 150,000 to 200,000 postal workers nationwide were eventually involved.

Mail travel shut down across the country. Business correspondence, Social Security checks, packages to the troops in

Vietnam, tax refunds, U.S. Census forms, and draft notices were not being delivered. The IRS could not receive the tax payments sent to it by mail. Important documents could not reach the stock exchange; the stock market fell. "A modern economy is sustained by an endless flow of carefully directed paper," wrote *Newsweek*. "The U.S. postal system . . . simply has no parallel in performing this vital function."

POST OFFICE LETTER CARRIERS IN NEW YORK STARTED A STRIKE IN MARCH 1970, CALLING FOR BETTER WAGES. THIS STRIKER CARRIES A SIGN THAT SHOWS ONE OF THEIR GRIEVANCES. MEMBERS OF CONGRESS HAD GIVEN THEMSELVES A RAISE OF 41 PERCENT (THE SIGN MISTAKENLY SAYS 50 PERCENT) WHILE THEY WERE CONSIDERING A RAISE OF 4 TO 5.4 PERCENT FOR POSTAL WORKERS. AT THE TIME OF THE STRIKE, WORKERS' WAGE INCREASE REMAINED AT ZERO.

The federal government refused to negotiate with the wildcat strikers. President Richard Nixon declared a state of emergency on March 22. Some 24,000 reserve troops, including the National Guard, showed up at the New York post office to sort and deliver 60 million pieces of mail.

PRESIDENT RICHARD NIXON CALLED IN TROOPS TO REPLACE STRIKING POSTAL WORKERS IN NEW YORK CITY. HERE, THEY TRY TO SORT MAIL, ALTHOUGH THEIR SPEED WAS MUCH SLOWER THAN THAT OF REGULAR EMPLOYEES. AFTER THREE DAYS, NIXON WITHDREW THEM, AND STRIKERS AGREED TO NEGOTIATE WITH THE FEDERAL GOVERNMENT.

Experienced postal clerks could place up to sixty letters a minute in a sorting pigeonhole. Untrained soldiers were confused and much slower. They did deliver some mail to businesses, though not to homes.

The troops left on March 25 when the government finally began negotiations with union leaders that day. The strikers agreed to stand down. With an agreement for a large salary increase—what eventually came to 14 percent more than what they had been making—the postal unions supported a new act reorganizing the Post Office. On August 12, 1970, Nixon signed the Postal Reorganization Act (PRA) into law.

The PRA transformed the United States Post Office Department into the United States Postal Service (USPS). In an attempt to make the postal system less political, Congress removed it from the president's executive cabinet. The act made it a corporation owned by the government. The postmaster general would no longer be appointed directly by the president. Congress would no longer provide operating funds. Both the government and postal leaders were optimistic that this change would make operating USPS more efficient. They believed that operating on a business model would create more income for the postal service, lower charges for customers, and improve service.

HOW THE NEW USPS WORKED

The PRA described USPS as "an independent establishment of the executive branch of the Government of the United States." While the government still has some control, it is run by a board of governors and top USPS managers. The board can have up to nine governors. They are appointed by the president and approved by the Senate. The governors choose the postmaster general, who then becomes a member of the board. Only the board of governors has the power to remove a postmaster general from office, not the president or Congress.

While the U.S. Post Office was largely run as a public service, the United States Postal Service is meant to run as a business. What it makes from postage sales and other services is supposed to cover its costs, with no additional money from Congress. These costs include paying the salaries of hundreds of thousands of postal workers. The postmaster general, the board of governors, and the Postal Regulatory Commission are in charge of management and policy. But the PRA did not give them final authority over how USPS is run or what it charges. Congress has the final say. Since

The board controls expenses and sets policy. The postmaster general manages the day-to-day operations of USPS. Any changes to the cost of postage for everything from letters to magazines to packages have to be approved by a Postal Regulatory Commission, which is separate from the board. The commission's five members are appointed by the president and confirmed by the Senate. The board of governors can accept, reject, or modify decisions made by the Postal Regulatory Commission.

The PRA, for the first time, gave postal unions the right to bargain for better pay, retirement benefits, and working conditions.

the president appoints the board of governors, who select the postmaster general, he also has significant influence over how USPS works.

The U.S. Postal Service, then, is not free, as a private business is, to make its own decisions about raising prices, buying equipment, hiring or cutting workers, or closing facilities that are not making a profit. Yet its mission, as established when it was the U.S. Post Office Department, remains the same: to provide the same level of service to every American. This is required even if it costs more to provide that service in some parts of the country than in others. But if it needs to serve areas that don't make a profit, how can it break even—bring in as much money as it spends—in order to support itself?

This might have been possible if the need for postal services and the cost for running USPS had remained the same. But from 1970 into the twenty-first century, the volume of mail USPS has had to process and deliver got bigger and bigger. Each item mailed brought in money. But to collect, process, and deliver it cost money too. USPS spent money on transportation and equipment, but the largest cost was paying postal workers. Between 1971 and 1975 alone, USPS granted three big pay raises to workers. Although USPS automated and updated equipment, which cut down on labor, it still had trouble keeping pace with the volume of mail.

Another important change was the number of items mailed first class (including letters, bills, greeting cards, postcards, and small packages) versus the number of pieces of marketing or "junk" mail.

By 2005, "junk" or marketing mail had overtaken the amount of First-Class Mail sent. Marketing mail is attractive to businesses because it can be sent at a discounted price. It is mailed in bulk and can be targeted to particular zip

WHAT THE POSTAL SERVICE DELIVERS

★ First-Class Mail, including anything in an envelope (letters, bills, checks, etc.), postcards, and packages weighing less than 13 ounces

★ Priority Mail, similar to First-Class Mail, but guaranteed for faster delivery (It costs the customer more.)

★ Priority Mail Express, similar to First-Class Mail, but guaranteed overnight delivery (It costs more than Priority Mail.)

★ Marketing mail, sometimes called "junk mail," includes flyers, circulars, advertising, and catalogs

★ Magazines, newspapers, and other periodicals

★ Media Mail, which includes printed, audio, and video material like books, CDs, DVDs, printed music, and 16mm or narrower film (Comic books cannot be sent by media mail because they are not considered to be educational, although any book or DVD can be sent by Media Mail even if it is not specifically educational.)

★ Freight and large packages via ground or air

A PILE OF MARKETING OR "JUNK" MAIL DELIVERED TO A SINGLE RESIDENT. BY 2005, MORE JUNK MAIL WAS BEING SENT THROUGH USPS THAN FIRST-CLASS MAIL. THE POSTAL SERVICE MAKES LESS MONEY PROCESSING AND DELIVERING A PIECE OF JUNK MAIL THAN IT DOES FROM A SINGLE LETTER.

codes to directly reach consumers who the business believes might be interested in a service or product. Marketing mail is cheaper to send per item than First-Class Mail. Although USPS is handling more and more of it, it is making less per item than it would if there had been an increase in letters and cards.

The internet and email have had a huge impact on what gets sent through USPS. In 1985, America Online (AOL) started the first electronic mail (email) service, and other services followed. With one click on a computer or cell phone or tablet, a message can be sent and received; it does not take days to be delivered. Many companies bill and consumers pay their bills online. This has created great competition for USPS.

A WOMAN USES HER LAPTOP COMPUTER TO SEND AND RECEIVE EMAIL. THE INCREASE IN THE USE OF EMAIL TO SEND MESSAGES AND LETTERS AND TO PAY BILLS HAS LED TO A DECREASE IN THE AMOUNT OF FIRST-CLASS MAIL SENT THROUGH USPS.

Since 1970, USPS has also had to compete more and more with private mail companies. These include FedEx and UPS, which promise faster delivery, although at a higher price. They have their own fleets of airplanes to transport packages. USPS has even contracted with them to fly U.S. mail.

By the twenty-first century, the USPS hybrid business/public service model was not working well. Congress—whose laws make the decisions about how the postal service runs—appears to be faced with two main choices.

One option is to completely privatize the postal service. It would become a private company, taken over by a competitive business. There would be no government funds to support it and no government regulations and oversight. It could raise prices as high as it wanted, not only to cover costs but to make a profit. It could close post offices that do not make money. It could cut down the number of employees working for it. It could even stop bargaining with unions for better pay and benefits for its workers. Supporters of privatization see USPS as a drain on taxpayers' money that will only increase with time.

What would this mean to Americans? Many customers already complain that postal prices are getting higher and higher. But the price to mail a letter or card or package with a private postal service would likely rise even more. Private Saturday delivery would certainly cost more, instead of being a regular postal day like any other. The postal "business" might be able to run more efficiently, but running efficiently sometimes winds up costing the public money. It also means that the labor force could be paid less.

PACKAGES MAKE UP A LARGE QUANTITY OF MAIL TODAY. HERE, BOXES PILE UP IN A WAREHOUSE. THEY REPRESENT A LARGE PART OF THE BUSINESS OF PRIVATE DELIVERY SERVICES AS WELL AS USPS.

No longer mandated by the government to serve everyone, a private post office, looking to make a profit, would likely underserve rural and scattered suburban areas. These areas cost more money to service. Some people might not have a postal facility near them at all, because these would not be profitable. Supporters of privatization point out—accurately—that many Americans, perhaps the majority, use the internet and email to pay bills and send personal messages. They don't use the mail except for packages. This assumes a lifestyle and an income that applies to everyone.

During the COVID-19 pandemic, when most children were schooled at home, it became clear that not all homes had the technology to do this well. Nearly 23 million Americans do not use the internet, a 2021 Pew survey found. They include older adults and families with low incomes. Surveys only consider those who answer their questions. There could well be more Americans not using the internet or who have to use it in public places, like libraries. In any case, there are a lot of people who depend only on the mail to deliver necessary items like prescription medications, bills, and benefit checks—even letters from loved ones—to their doors.

AN INNOVATIVE SERVICE: POSTAL BANKING

The U.S. Post Office has a history of reaching out to underserved populations. In the late nineteenth and early twentieth centuries, immigrants were pouring into America from Europe. In their home countries they could put their savings in government-regulated banks, many of them postal banks. In the United States, the South and West had very few banks for anyone. In 1910, Congress created the United States Postal Savings System to provide this service through its network of post offices.

Postal savings banks did not immediately take off in the western and southern states. But immigrants to the Northeast flocked to use them. They felt that their money was safe in a government-sponsored bank. The Post Office advertised its service in twenty-four languages. It gave information to passengers as they disembarked from ships at the busiest ports. In 1915, 70 percent of all deposits in postal savings banks were made by immigrants, although they represented less than 15 percent of the American population.

Postal savings banks were created to encourage even those with low incomes not to hide their money under beds or to bury it in the backyard but to invest it for themselves and the American economy. Depositors earned 2 percent interest a year, building on their savings. Even a young person—anyone ten years or older—could open a postal savings bank account. The minimum deposit was only $1. At first, $500 was the most a person could have in an account. The amount was kept low so that postal savings banks would not compete with private commercial banks. This was raised to $2,500 in 1918.

By 1934, postal savings banks held $1.2 billion. These banks made up 10 percent of all banks in the country. In 1940, the Post Office began accepting deposits by mail. After the United States entered World War II in 1941, this helped soldiers fighting overseas to bank at home. Postal banks were very successful at selling millions of dollars' worth of war bonds to help finance the war.

As the economy improved after World War II, Americans turned more to commercial banks. These banks paid higher interest rates. Safeguards like the Federal Deposit Insurance Corporation (FDIC), put in place during the Great Depression, ensured that savings would be safe even if a bank was forced to close. Because fewer Americans depended on it, the postal savings bank system ended in 1966.

DEPOSITORS STAND IN LINE AT A POSTAL SAVINGS BANK DEPOSITORY WINDOW, READY TO ADD TO OR DRAW FROM THEIR SAVINGS ACCOUNTS. POSTAL SAVINGS BANKS OFFERED AMERICANS WITH LOW INCOMES A WAY TO KEEP THEIR MONEY SAFE.

The second option would be to keep USPS truly a public service. That is how it was conceived by the Founding Fathers and operated for nearly two hundred years. It's not that Congress did not complain of its cost during all this time. It did. But political leaders felt that what was most important was binding the country together. By paying private companies to transport mail—whether by stagecoach, by railroad, or by airplane—it subsidized the growth of these industries and was vital to their development. This cost to the postal service was of great benefit to the country and its businesses. It is a fact almost always ignored when leaders talk about the postal service being a drain on taxpayer money.

As a public service, USPS would be subsidized by taxpayers' money. It would automatically be part of the overall federal budget. It could still make money by, for example, raising the price of stamps and services like Priority Mail Express. It could streamline its management. But it would not be expected to be totally self-supporting—just like all the other federal departments and branches are not, including the Army, the Navy, the Air Force, the Marines, the Department of Homeland Security, the Food and Drug

Administration, the Justice Department, the FBI, the Centers for Disease Control (CDC), and dozens and dozens of other departments, bureaus, and agencies. These provide services Americans expect as part of living in this country. If USPS became a private business, it would not be the same as the familiar and popular service that has connected all parts of the United States for more than two hundred years.

6

AFRICAN AMERICANS IN THE POST OFFICE

Before the Civil War, enslaved Black people were sometimes used to carry mail from place to place. They also worked for mail delivery contractors. "If the inhabitants . . . should deem their letters safe with a faithful black, I should not refuse him [the ability to carry mail]," wrote Postmaster General Timothy Pickering to a Maryland resident in 1794.

POSTMASTER GENERAL TIMOTHY PICKERING IS SHOWN IN THIS 1806 ENGRAVING. HE WAS APPOINTED BY PRESIDENT GEORGE WASHINGTON IN 1791 AND SERVED UNTIL 1795, WHEN HE BECAME SECRETARY OF STATE. AN OPPONENT OF SLAVERY, PICKERING THOUGHT THAT FREE BLACK PEOPLE SHOULD BE ALLOWED TO CARRY THE MAIL.

Pickering was against slavery. He favored allowing free Black people to carry the mail. To those who objected to his policy, he replied, "If you admitted a negro to be a *man*, the difficulty [in employing him to carry the mail] would cease."

Joseph Habersham, the postmaster general who followed Pickering, defended the policy of employing African Americans. In an 1801 letter to the postmaster of Frankfort, Kentucky, he noted that using enslaved people to carry the mail "was generally allowed in the Southern States by my predecessors in office. I make no objection to it especially as it came within my knowledge that slaves in general are more trustworthy than that class of white men who will perform such services—the stages . . . [on] the Main Line are driven by Slaves & most of the Contractors employ them as mail carriers in the Southern States."

But a continuing rebellion by enslaved people in Haiti against France (1791–1804) made white people anxious. They were afraid that enslaved people in the United States would rebel. The Haitian conflict was still raging in 1802 when Postmaster General Gideon Granger wrote to the Senate chairman on the Post Office that "after the scenes which St. Domingo [Haiti] has exhibited to the world, we cannot be too cautious . . . The most active and intelligent [slaves] are

employed as post riders . . . By traveling from day to day, and hourly mixing with people . . . they will acquire information. They will learn that a man's rights do not depend on his color. They will, in time, become teachers to their brethren."

In May 1802, Congress passed an act that stated: "After the 1st day of November next, no other than a free white person shall be employed in carrying the mail of the United States, on any post-roads, either as a post-rider or driver of a carriage carrying the mails." The fine for a white person hiring an African American to deliver mail was $50. In 1828, Postmaster General John McLean said that Black people might be allowed to unload heavy mailbags from stage-coaches as long as they were supervised by a white person.

African Americans were banned by law from transport-ing mail until March 3, 1865—one month prior to the end of the Civil War. The act passed by Congress declared that "no person, by reason of color, shall be disqualified from employ-ment in carrying the mails, and all acts and parts of acts establishing such disqualification . . . are hereby repealed."

AMERICANS WERE ALARMED BY AN ONGOING REBELLION OF ENSLAVED PEOPLE IN HAITI AGAINST FRANCE IN 1801. THIS LITHOGRAPH FROM THAT YEAR SHOWS A HAITIAN MILITARY OFFICER WITH A COPY OF THE COUNTRY'S NEW CONSTITUTION AND THE WORDS "LIBERTY" AND "EQUALITY" IN FRENCH. FEARING THAT DELIVERING MAIL WOULD GIVE ENSLAVED AMERICANS A WAY TO COMMUNICATE, CONGRESS FORBADE BLACK PEOPLE TO CARRY IT IN 1802.

WILLIAM NELL, FIRST AFRICAN AMERICAN CLERK

Although the ban on hiring African Americans was not officially lifted until 1865, Boston's postmaster, John Palfrey, defied the law. He made William Cooper Nell a clerk in the Boston post office in 1861. (Nell is not listed in the records of the Post Office until 1863, but newspaper articles and letters indicate the earlier year.) Nell was an abolitionist and journalist. He wrote two short books about the service of Black people during the American Revolution and the War of 1812. They are considered the first published histories by an African American.

In 1873, Nell wrote to abolitionist William Lloyd Garrison, with whom he had worked, that he was "the first colored man employed about the United States Mail." He was, in fact, the first known Black American civilian appointed to any federal job. Nell told Garrison that he had "never lost a day from sickness or any cause." He stayed in the job until his death in 1874.

WILLIAM COOPER NELL WAS APPOINTED AS A CLERK IN THE BOSTON POST OFFICE BEFORE THE BAN ON AFRICAN AMERICANS WORKING AT THE POST OFFICE WAS LIFTED. HE WAS AN EARLY ABOLITIONIST AND WORKED TO TRANSPORT ENSLAVED PEOPLE FROM THE SOUTH ON THE UNDERGROUND RAILROAD. NELL HELD HIS JOB AT THE POST OFFICE FOR THIRTEEN YEARS.

The first African American appointed as a postmaster was James W. Mason, in 1867. He ran the post office at Sunnyside, Arkansas. Postmaster was a relatively prestigious position. Mason later became an Arkansas state senator and served as a county judge and a county sheriff.

In 1869, William H. Carney became a letter carrier in New Bedford, Massachusetts. Carney was a Civil War veteran who fought with the 54th Massachusetts Colored Infantry Regiment, an all-Black unit headed by a white commander. While trying to breach the Confederate stronghold of Fort Wagner in South Carolina, most of the soldiers were killed. Carney survived. When the regiment's standard-bearer was shot and dropped the U.S. flag, Carney lifted it up. He was the first African American awarded a Congressional

CIVIL WAR VETERAN WILLIAM H. CARNEY WORKED AS A MAIL CARRIER IN NEW BEDFORD, MASSACHUSETTS, FOR THIRTY-TWO YEARS. HE WAS THE FIRST AFRICAN AMERICAN AWARDED THE CONGRESSIONAL MEDAL OF HONOR. HERE, HE IS SHOWN IN 1900, THE YEAR HE RECEIVED THE MEDAL, MORE THAN THIRTY-FIVE YEARS AFTER HIS HEROIC ACTION DURING THE WAR.

Medal of Honor, though not until 1900. Carney worked as a letter carrier for thirty-two years. When he delivered the mail, he often wore his Union Army greatcoat over his postal uniform.

Carney was not the only Black Civil War veteran to work for the Post Office. Filled with pride from their service, African American veterans looked for employment that was stable and offered dignity. Denied other jobs because of their race, they were accepted by the Post Office. Several became postmasters in cities and towns. Over a dozen served in the predominantly Black towns that were settled by freedmen after the Civil War. More than three hundred African Americans worked as mail carriers in the second half of the nineteenth century.

After the Civil War, three amendments to the Constitution were passed to guarantee the rights of African Americans. The Thirteenth Amendment (adopted in 1865) abolished slavery. The Fourteenth Amendment (adopted in 1868) made African Americans citizens of the United States and promised equal protection under the law. The Fifteenth Amendment (adopted in 1870) gave African American men the right to vote. The United States government followed a policy called Reconstruction. Black people were elected as federal, state, and local officials. They had some protection against discrimination.

But the southern states resisted these changes. They began to pass their own laws, limiting Black freedom. For example, a Black man without a job could be arrested for vagrancy and sent to work under the same conditions as an enslaved person. After Reconstruction ended in 1877, the federal government no longer intervened to protect the rights of Black Americans. More laws in the South followed to promote a policy of segregation. These "Jim Crow" laws— whether official laws or "unwritten laws"—separated Black and white Americans in public places, housing, schools, and jobs. To keep segregation in place, white people frequently used intimidation and violence. This was true in northern and western states as well as in the South.

SEGREGATION LAWS IN THE SOUTH, AS WELL AS RACIAL DISCRIMINATION IN THE REST OF THE UNITED STATES, MADE IT DIFFICULT FOR AFRICAN AMERICANS IN THE EARLY HALF OF THE TWENTIETH CENTURY TO FIND GOOD, STABLE JOBS. THIS SIGN, "WE CATER TO WHITE TRADE ONLY," IN THE WINDOW OF AN OHIO RESTAURANT IN 1938, SHOWS HOW JIM CROW PRACTICES SEPARATED BLACK AND WHITE AMERICANS.

African Americans who wanted to work for the Post Office felt the effects of this discrimination and violence. The appointment of Frazier Baker as postmaster of Lake City, South Carolina, in 1897, enraged the mostly white town. A mob set fire to Baker's home, which was also the post office and therefore federal property. Although his wife and several children escaped, Baker and a young daughter were killed. The guilty parties in many crimes like this were never arrested. In Baker's case, eleven men were charged and brought to trial. The jury found three not guilty and could not agree on whether the other eight were guilty or not. None of the accused ever went to prison.

However, the Pendleton Civil Service Act of 1883 (sponsored by Senator George Pendleton of Ohio) affected African Americans in a more positive way. Before this act was passed, federal jobs, including all Post Office jobs, were filled under what was called "patronage" or the "spoils system." This meant that whichever political party gained the most power in state and national elections could fire federal

THE STORY OF AFRICAN AMERICAN FRAZIER BAKER, APPOINTED POSTMASTER OF LAKE CITY, SOUTH CAROLINA, IN 1897, ENDED IN TRAGEDY. A WHITE MOB SET FIRE TO BAKER'S HOUSE THE FOLLOWING YEAR, KILLING HIM AND ONE OF HIS DAUGHTERS. THIS PHOTO, TAKEN IN 1899, SHOWS THE FAMILY THAT SURVIVED: HIS WIFE, LAVINIA RUSSELL BAKER (*FIRST ROW, SECOND FROM LEFT*), AND FIVE OF THEIR CHILDREN.

"STAGECOACH MARY" FIELDS

Born enslaved, Mary Fields was the first African American woman to get a Post Office contract to be a Star Route carrier, in 1895. She was already in her sixties but six feet tall and still strong and tough. She was able to handle the rough roads of Montana. Her route ran from the town of Cascade to St. Peter's Mission, some fifteen miles each way. In the eight years she was a Star Route carrier, Fields never missed a day of work. She was known for being extremely reliable as well as independent.

She was called "Stagecoach Mary" because she usually used a wagon and horse to deliver the mail. She also traveled on her mule, Moses, when blizzards threatened to stop her. When the snow was too high, she used snowshoes to walk

workers from the losing party. The winning party then filled the positions with people who had been loyal to it. The Pendleton Civil Service Act abolished this system. Applicants had to take an exam. They were hired on ability or merit. Black college graduates, especially, benefited from the change.

But Black postal applicants came up against the "rule of three." (From 1883 to 1888, this was the "rule of four.") Those hiring for a federal job could pick one of the top three people

to her destination. She carried a revolver and a rifle to protect herself from bandits and wolves. She had a reputation for being fearless. One of her greatest services was to bring mail to and from isolated miners' cabins, helping them to quickly process their claims.

"STAGECOACH MARY" FIELDS WAS BORN INTO SLAVERY. AFTER EMANCIPATION, SHE HELD SEVERAL JOBS, INCLUDING WORKING FOR A CONVENT OF NUNS IN OHIO AND LATER MONTANA. THERE, IN 1895, SHE BECAME THE FIRST AFRICAN AMERICAN WOMAN EMPLOYED AS A STAR ROUTE CARRIER, THE SAME YEAR THIS PHOTO WAS TAKEN. SHE FEARLESSLY TRAVELED THE RUGGED ROUTE, FENDING OFF WILD ANIMALS AND BANDITS, FOR EIGHT YEARS.

who had scored the highest on the civil service exam. They could, for example, choose the third person, who scored 90, instead of the first, who scored 100. Employers often had some knowledge of who had applied. Even if an African American received the highest score, she or he might not be hired.

While working for the Post Office became an accepted way for African Americans to find steady employment and move up into the middle class, it was still very difficult for

WHO'S GOT MAIL?

a Black person to be hired for a management position no matter how qualified he or she was. If an African American did get such a job, discrimination stopped him or her from advancing to a higher position in a business, company, or federal job, including the Post Office.

Therefore, "comparatively well educated negroes are willing, indeed, glad, to take minor clerkships under the government, places which do not appeal to white men of ability for the simple reason that the white man can do better," read a 1908 article in the *Washington Post*. The reason a white man could "do better" was that he would not be discriminated against because of his color. "The consequence is that the most capable of the negroes compete with whites of at best only mediocre ability," concluded the *Post*.

The federal government usually offered better employment than the

AFRICAN AMERICANS WERE HIRED AS CITY MAIL CARRIERS STARTING IN 1869. HERE, A BLACK CARRIER DELIVERS MAIL TO THE S. J. GILPIN SHOE STORE IN RICHMOND, VIRGINIA, CIRCA 1899.

private sector. In 1902, President Theodore Roosevelt wrote, "It is and should be my consistent policy in every State, where their numbers warranted it, to recognize colored men of good repute and standing in making appointments to office . . . I can not consent to take the position that the door of hope—the door of opportunity—is to be shut upon any man, no matter how worthy, purely upon the grounds of race or color."

By 1912, about 4,000 African Americans worked for the Post Office. They had jobs, but most often these were the lower-paying ones. Few African Americans were supervisors.

BLACK AND WHITE POSTAL CLERKS WORKED TOGETHER IN THE RAILWAY MAIL SERVICE WITH FEW COMPLAINTS. IN THIS 1930 PHOTO THEY ARE WORKING SIDE BY SIDE. BUT DURING WOODROW WILSON'S PRESIDENCY (1913–1921), POSTMASTER GENERAL ALBERT BURLESON INTRODUCED SEGREGATION INTO POST OFFICE WORKPLACES. DURING THIS TIME, BLACK AND WHITE CUSTOMERS OFTEN HAD TO USE SEPARATE WINDOWS TO COLLECT THEIR MAIL.

THREATS TO BLACK POSTAL WORKERS

African American Minnie M. Cox had served as postmaster of Indianola, Mississippi, as early as 1891. In 1902, white residents of Indianola forced her to resign. President Theodore Roosevelt would not accept her resignation. He ordered that the Indianola post office be closed. The town had to get its mail from Greenville, twenty-five miles away, until 1904, when Cox's term expired. The threat of violence against her was so great that she fled for her safety in early January 1903, although technically she remained

They were far more likely to be mail carriers than clerks or postmasters. But they were not segregated where they worked. For example, they worked side by side with white people as clerks for the Railway Mail Service.

After Woodrow Wilson became president in 1913, however, some federal offices were segregated. Wilson's postmaster general, Albert S. Burleson, whose father had been an officer in the Confederate Army, was one of the first to raise the issue. At a meeting of Wilson's cabinet, the Navy secretary recorded that Burleson "was anxious to seg-regate white and negro employees in all Departments of the

the postmaster. The American press took up her story. "Mrs. Minnie Cox, Postmistress of Indianola—A Faithful and Efficient Official Driven from Office by Southern White Brutes," read a headline in the *Cleveland Gazette* in February.

In another case, Roosevelt's postmaster general, Henry C. Payne, stopped the delivery of mail in part of rural Tennessee when the Black carrier was threatened by armed men. "When the people in the localities which object to the appointees of this department are willing to accept them and permit them to perform their duties unmolested these sections will be given the benefit of the mails," Payne told the *Chicago Tribune*.

Government . . . [H]e believed segregation was best for the negro and best for the Service." Burleson was particularly upset about the situation in Railway Mail Service cars. He called it "intolerable" because African Americans drank from the same glasses and used the same towels in the same restrooms as white people.

Not only did Burleson separate Black and white people in their workplaces, but many Black people lost their jobs or were demoted. African American customers who wanted to mail letters now had to go to segregated windows in post offices. This was true not only in the South but elsewhere in

UNIONS AGAINST SEGREGATION

To protest Burleson's discriminatory policies, the National Alliance of Postal and Federal Employees was formed in October 1913. It was organized by a group of Black railway mail clerks. Other postal unions did not allow African Americans to join.

P. M. E. Hill spoke to fellow union members in 1917 about widespread discrimination: "I regret that I must arise as an American citizen and a member of the greatest organization in the world [the U.S. Post Office] which seemingly is purely

the country. By 1914, anyone applying for a civil service job, including a job in the Post Office, had to submit a photo with his or her application as well as pass an exam. There was no need for an interview to know a person's color.

Despite this, the number of Black workers continued to rise, although the number of Black supervisors or clerks remained low. Seventy percent of workers at the Chicago Post Office in 1930 were Black. But only 28 percent of clerks and 5 percent of foremen were Black.

In the 1940s, the federal government made some effort to stop discrimination. Both Presidents Franklin D. Roosevelt

democratic and stands for all men, to defend myself as a black man to be separated from other Americans just because I was born black. . . I was in the Spanish-American War. . . I have a boy now who is in the trenches in France [fighting in World War I]. . . I believe in the proposition of all men up and no man down, and this is wrong."

In 1923, the National Alliance invited all those, Black or white, who worked for the Post Office to become members. It integrated the union long before President John Kennedy issued an executive order in 1962 banning unions of federal workers from segregating by race.

and Harry Truman issued several executive orders calling for equal opportunity. The reality was different. "A city where a Negro does not have to contend for his rights in America would be a miracle city and I have as yet to hear of such a city," observed Raymond A. C. Young, a black letter carrier in Baltimore, in 1944.

Fair employment and raises to better-paid jobs depended on the attitude of the people making the decisions in each individual post office. In New Orleans in 1949, break rooms were segregated. In Birmingham, Montgomery, and Mobile, Alabama, post offices had separate restrooms and break

IN THE 1900S, AN INCREASING NUMBER OF AFRICAN AMERICANS FOUND WORK AT THE POST OFFICE, BUT THE MAJORITY OF THEM HELD LABORING JOBS; VERY FEW WERE IN MANAGEMENT. THIS 1938 PHOTO OF A LOADING PLATFORM IN THE WASHINGTON, DC, POST OFFICE SHOWS A BLACK POSTAL WORKER PILING UP MAILBAGS WHILE A WHITE EMPLOYEE APPEARS TO LOOK ON.

rooms. In 1959, 66 percent of the workers at the Washington, DC, post office were African American. Only 15 percent of these employees were supervisors.

In the early 1960s, Black Americans began to be appointed to more positions as supervisors. Christopher C. Scott became a deputy to the assistant postmaster general for transportation in 1961. This was the highest-ranking position any African American had ever held in the postal service. In 1964, Leslie N. Shaw was appointed as postmaster of Los Angeles, the first Black postmaster of a large American city.

The legal cases, marches, demonstrations, and protests of the civil rights movement led to the passage of the Civil Rights Act of 1964. President Lyndon B. Johnson signed it into law. This law banned segregation in public places. The Voting Rights Act of 1965 made it illegal for states to prevent Black Americans from voting by making registration difficult, using literacy tests, and requiring payment of a poll tax. These were important breakthroughs, but they did not end discrimination.

Yet African Americans still looked to the Post Office for stable jobs. "It is important to note that most of the women coming into the PO [Post Office] are Negroes," reported a postal union newspaper in 1966. "Reflecting the conditions in the American economy and the unfair treatment that they have received on the 'outside' down through the years, these women come into the Federal government hoping that they will get a 'fair shake.'"

By 2021, more African Americans were in management, including as postmasters in large cities. Garry Simmons spent thirty-two years working for USPS. He credited his job with providing a better life for his family. "I was able to raise them, help pay for my son's college education, provide a good middle-class lifestyle for us," he said in an interview. Similar stories have been told.

HEMAN SWEATT: POSTAL WORKERS FIGHT FOR CIVIL RIGHTS

Many Black postal workers were active in the civil rights movement of the 1950s and 1960s. One of these was Heman Marion Sweatt, who delivered mail in Houston from about 1938 to 1947. In 1946, when he applied for admission to the University of Texas Law School, he was rejected because he was African American. With the help of the National Association for the Advancement of Colored People (NAACP), he sued the university.

In 1950, the U.S. Supreme Court ruled in *Sweatt v. Painter* that the university had to admit him to the law school.

Women, like African Americans, had to fight discrimination. But, like Black Americans, they broke down barriers, culminating in the appointment of the first female postmaster general, Megan Brennan, in 2014. The story of women in the Post Office exemplifies the handicaps most women faced in the nineteenth and first half of the twentieth century.

The court said that the state could not provide a separate law school for Black students equal to the quality of the education Sweatt could get at the University of Texas. The decision was an important challenge to the "separate but equal" doctrine used to justify segregation. It was made four years before the Supreme Court ruled in *Brown v. Board of Education* that separate schools were in fact never equal.

HEMAN SWEATT HAD BEEN A MAIL CARRIER IN HOUSTON, TEXAS, FOR NINE YEARS WHEN HE APPLIED TO THE UNIVERSITY OF TEXAS LAW SCHOOL. HE HAD ALREADY EARNED A BACHELOR OF ARTS DEGREE AND HAD DONE POSTGRADUATE WORK AT THE UNIVERSITY OF MICHIGAN, SO HIS QUALIFICATIONS WERE NOT IN DOUBT. TEXAS DENIED HIM ADMISSION BECAUSE OF HIS RACE, LEADING TO THE SUPREME COURT CASE *SWEATT V. PAINTER*, WHICH REQUIRED THE UNIVERSITY TO ADMIT HIM.

Harriet Tubman

Black Heritage USA 13c

AFRICAN AMERICANS FIRST APPEARED ON STAMPS BEGINNING IN 1940, WHEN EDUCATOR BOOKER T. WASHINGTON WAS HONORED. THIS 1978 COMMEMORATIVE STAMP SHOWS HARRIET TUBMAN, WHO RESCUED MANY ENSLAVED PEOPLE FROM THE SOUTH. SHE IS THE FIRST AFRICAN AMERICAN WOMAN TO APPEAR ON A STAMP AND THE FIRST PERSON IN THE 1978 BLACK HERITAGE STAMP SERIES.

7 WOMEN IN THE POST OFFICE

Postal carrier Etta E. Bolton, of Mobile, Alabama, "was driving her mail wagon across a swollen stream over a rickety bridge, when, just as she reached the middle, the structure gave way . . .

"With great presence of mind and exceptional pluck she managed to extricate herself from the debris and the struggling horse and gain the shore.

"The wagon, horse and contents of the vehicle were doing their best to make an end to all, but Miss Bolton plunged again into the torrent . . . Nearly exhausted, she finally gained the bank, having saved every sack and pouch of mail."

The *Atlanta Constitution* of March 3, 1905, featured this story of a day in the life of a female rural postal carrier.

From its beginnings in the eighteenth century, however,

the Post Office did not favor hiring women. They were considered too weak and delicate for some jobs, like hauling mailbags or driving over rough terrain. Yet, in the late 1890s, some eighteen women had contract routes, or Star Routes. The first to get one was Polly Martin in 1860. She drove between Attleboro and South Attleboro, Massachusetts. Her wagon could carry six passengers as well as mail. In 1884, Martin told the *Boston Daily Globe* that traveling "was pretty tough sometimes, in the winter . . . Many a time I . . . got out and dug the horse out of the drifts."

"STAGECOACH MARY" FIELDS WAS ONE OF THE FIRST WOMEN TO DELIVER MAIL AS A STAR ROUTE CARRIER. WOMEN SERVED AS POSTMASTERS IN THE EIGHTEENTH CENTURY, BUT IT WAS NOT UNTIL THE LATE NINETEENTH CENTURY THAT THEY WERE HIRED AS CARRIERS.

After Rural Free Delivery started in 1896, some women became carriers on these routes. The 1899 report of the postmaster general mentioned that "on at least two routes there are girl carriers, and they are as unflagging in their devotion to the service as the men and as efficient." One of them was Sarah Burks, a former enslaved person who transported mail in Arizona on a "wild and desolate and God-forsaken" route, carrying a pistol and revolver to protect her from bandits. The first known female city carriers were hired in Washington, DC, in 1917. World War I had depleted the ranks of male carriers. The practice spread to other cities. But when World War I ended and men returned, almost all the women were let go from their jobs. The same thing occurred after World War II. By 1955, only ninety-five women remained as city carriers.

The Post Office was reluctant to appoint women as postmasters as well. Postmasters ran individual post offices in cities and towns. Among their duties were "the receipt and dispatch of the mails at all times day or night; the constant watch necessary to be kept over the conduct of contractors and carriers . . . ; the superintendence of mail service generally within the vicinity of the office; the pursuit and arrest of mail depredators; and prosecutions for violations of the Post

Office laws," according to Cave Johnson, postmaster general from 1845 to 1849. Johnson explained that, because of this, "it has not been the practice of the Department to appoint females . . . at the larger offices; the duties required of them are . . . often of a character that ladies could not be expected to perform . . . [They] could not with propriety be exacted of a lady."

ALTHOUGH ALMOST ALL WOMEN CITY CARRIERS WERE LET GO AFTER WORLD WAR I, THE POST OFFICE USED THIS PHOTO OF OPERA STAR MERLE ALCOCK TO PROMOTE USING A NEW STYLE STREET COLLECTION MAILBOX IN THE 1920S.

MARY KATHERINE GODDARD

Considered the first woman postmaster in colonial America, Mary Katherine Goddard (1738–1816) began the job in 1775 in Baltimore. She held the position throughout the Revolutionary War and into the first years of the new United States.

Goddard's father had been the colonial postmaster of New London, Connecticut. Her brother established the *Maryland Journal* in Baltimore, where he also served as postmaster. Goddard ran the newspaper from 1774 to 1784. She was the first person to publish a copy of the Declaration of Independence with all the signers' signatures, in 1777.

Goddard successfully managed the newspaper and the post office. She made sacrifices to keep the mail going. "At her own [risk, she]

MARY KATHERINE GODDARD WAS LIKELY THE FIRST WOMAN TO HOLD A FEDERAL JOB UNDER THE REVOLUTIONARY WAR GOVERNMENT: SHE WAS APPOINTED BALTIMORE'S POSTMASTER IN 1775. IN 1789, POSTMASTER GENERAL SAMUEL OSGOOD WANTED TO GIVE HER JOB TO A MAN. SHE APPEALED TO CONGRESS TO KEEP HER JOB, IN A PETITION SHOWN HERE, BUT WAS FORCED TO STEP DOWN AFTER FOURTEEN YEARS OF SERVICE.

advanced hard money to defray the Charges of Post Riders for many years, when they were not to be procured on any other terms," she wrote in a letter to President George Washington in 1789. Goddard sent this letter because she was being removed from the job by Washington's postmaster general, Samuel Osgood.

Although Goddard had been Baltimore's postmaster for fourteen years, Osgood wanted to replace her with a man who had no postal experience. She sent a petition praising her work to Osgood. It was signed by 235 Baltimore citizens who believed she should keep the job. Osgood responded that he was expanding the duties of the postmaster to include travel to smaller post offices south of Baltimore. He did not think a woman could handle this. Goddard then appealed to President Washington. She wrote that she had "been discharged from her Office, without any imputation of the least fault, and without any previous official notice." She protested that "the whole of her Labour & Industry in establishing the Office was necessarily unrewarded." Washington backed his postmaster general. "I have uniformly avoided interfering with any appointments which do not require my official agency," he wrote to Goddard.

The male candidate took over the Baltimore post office. After losing an appeal to the United States House and Senate, Goddard stepped down in 1790 and ran a bookshop in the city for the next twenty years.

Nevertheless, a handful of women did serve in this position in the eighteenth and early nineteenth centuries. It was common for these women to be widows. Eight women were listed as postmasters in the Post Office's *Official Register* in 1816. By 1862, some 411 women worked as postmasters. About 28,500 men held the same job.

During the Civil War, with many men at the front, women began to be employed as clerks at Post Office headquarters in Washington, DC. They first worked in the Dead Letter Office. This office handled letters that could not be delivered because the addresses were unreadable or the recipients had moved. The clerks' job was to figure out a way to find

MARY CLARKE WATSON, SHOWN HERE CIRCA 1875, WAS THE POSTMASTER OF JAMESTOWN, RHODE ISLAND. APPOINTED IN 1880, WHEN SHE WAS FIFTY-SEVEN, SHE SERVED FOR EIGHT YEARS. SHE ALSO SERVED AS UNOFFICIAL TOWN CLERK FOR SIX YEARS. HER SON WAS THE OFFICIAL APPOINTEE, SINCE WOMEN COULD NOT HOLD THAT OFFICE.

the recipients or return these letters to the senders. In 1862, some ten women were hired. By 1865, female clerks at the headquarters outnumbered men, thirty-eight to seven. They were always paid less than men. Some who employed them saw this as the advantage of hiring women.

WOMEN MADE THEIR FIRST BIG BREAKTHROUGH AS FEDERAL POSTAL WORKERS AT THE WASHINGTON, DC, POSTAL HEADQUARTERS DURING THE CIVIL WAR. THEY WERE ASSIGNED TO THE DEAD LETTER OFFICE, WHERE THEY PROCESSED MAIL THAT COULD NOT BE DELIVERED BECAUSE THE ADDRESS WAS UNCLEAR. IF THEY COULD DECIPHER THE ADDRESS, THE LETTER WAS SENT ON. THE NUMBER OF WOMEN WORKING AT THE OFFICE QUICKLY SURPASSED THE NUMBER OF MEN. HERE, THEY WORK AT DESKS, WHILE A STANDING MALE SUPERVISOR LOOKS ON.

PATTI LYLE COLLINS, "PRESIDING GENIUS"

Of all those who worked in the Dead Letter Office in Washington, DC, Patti Lyle Collins was the only one who became a legend in her own time. She began work there in the early 1880s, when women and retired clergymen manned the office. Both were considered more honest than the average man so that they would not steal money found in an opened letter. Collins was said to review about a thousand letters a day with unreadable addresses.

PATTI LYLE COLLINS BEGAN WORK AT THE DEAD LETTER OFFICE IN THE EARLY 1880S. SHE WAS KNOWN FOR HER REMARKABLE ABILITY TO FIGURE OUT ADDRESSES THAT NO ONE ELSE COULD READ. HER SKILL RELIED PARTLY ON HER EXCELLENT MEMORY. SHE KNEW THE NAMES OF HUNDREDS OF STREETS IN MANY CITIES, SO SHE COULD MAKE AN EDUCATED GUESS ABOUT WHAT HAD BEEN WRITTEN—AND SHE WAS MOST OFTEN CORRECT.

Women worked other jobs in the Post Office headquarters as well. By 1879, they served in 19 percent of these jobs, and all fifty-five clerks in the Dead Letter Office were female. A few had special jobs and were paid more, like Annie

The *Ladies Home Journal* applauded her as the "presiding genius" in 1893. She was called "the expert puzzle solver" and "little less than a wizard."

Collins could read six languages. She had an astonishing knowledge of family names and place names—right down to the names of city streets, geographic terms, and handwriting styles. One of her most impressive talents was to translate garbled or badly spelled place names. She correctly identified "Tossy Tanner, Tx," as Corsicana, Texas; "Lacy Jane, Kansas," as La Cygne, Kansas; and "Reikzhieer, Stiejt Kanedeka," as Roxbury, Connecticut.

The 1893 *Ladies Home Journal* article described some of her many victories: "Picking up an envelope addressed to 3133 East Maryland Street, with no city or state given, Mrs. Collins knew that while many cities had 'Maryland' streets, only in Indianapolis [Indiana] did the numbers go as high as 3133."

"A letter to a law firm at 'Jerry Rescue Block, N.Y.,' made its way to Syracuse [New York] because Mrs. Collins knew the city was the scene of the 1851 rescue from jail of an enslaved fugitive, William Henry, who called himself 'Jerry.'"

Driver. She spoke ten languages and was a translator in the Office of Foreign Mails. But most women did the same jobs as men, and always for less pay.

Female postal clerks were expected to work with modesty

and decorum. "The women of the Department . . . are good and true," wrote Marshall Cushing in his 1893 history of the Post Office. "There is one, perhaps, who meddles in the politics of her division . . . but it is not one in a hundred, and all the rest work very demurely, purifying the rooms they work in . . . They are the kind of women a son or brother likes to respect and love."

Although a few men saw the presence of a gentlewoman as an attractive asset, women were usually seen as taking jobs that a man should hold. In 1899, an assistant postmaster general decreed that if a female clerk married a man who was a postal clerk, she should lose her job. Having married, she would have no need to support herself. In 1902, Postmaster General Henry Payne ruled that "a married woman will not be appointed to a classified position . . . and a classified woman in the postal service who shall change her name by marriage will not be reappointed." Clerk positions were placed in a higher class or category than other postal jobs. This ban lasted until 1921.

In 1918, Katherine Stinson was the first woman to carry airmail, from Chicago to New York. It wasn't until 1934, however, that Helen Richey became the first known woman to regularly pilot the mail. Her route went between

KATHERINE STINSON STANDS BESIDE HER CURTISS-STINSON SPECIAL BIPLANE, WHICH SHE FLEW TO RAISE FUNDS FOR THE RED CROSS DURING WORLD WAR I. STINSON WAS THE FIRST WOMAN TO OFFICIALLY TRANSPORT THE U.S. MAIL IN 1918, FROM CHICAGO TO NEW YORK.

Washington, DC, and Detroit. "I've done a lot of flying, but I'll never forget that first trip because it was my first time as a pilot of a regular airliner with the safety of a lot of passengers and Uncle Sam's mail in my hands," she told a newspaper. Richey flew for Central Airlines (later part of United Airlines), which had a Post Office contract. She had competed with eight men to get the job. But she was denied membership in a pilots' union and ordered by the federal Bureau of Air Commerce not to fly in bad weather, as men were allowed to do. Richey left the job in less than a year.

KATHERINE STINSON, AVIATOR

"Katherine Stinson, the aviatrix, who left Chicago this morning to fly to New York, carrying government mail, damaged her airplane while attempting a landing two miles north of the city at 6:40 this evening," reported the *Washington Post* on May 24, 1918. "The machine overturned just as it reached the ground, smashing the propeller and damaging one of the wings. Miss Stinson was uninjured." Stinson had wanted to make the trip in one day to break the world's nonstop distance record. But she did break two other records. "Having covered the 783 miles from Chicago to this city in ten hours, Miss Stinson bettered

Even in the second half of the twentieth century, women made slow advances in the Post Office. In the 1960s, some facilities still had no dedicated women's restrooms, and women had no standard uniforms as there were for men.

Women were also slow to move into top management positions. In 1979, only about 2.8 percent of jobs in the Postal Career Executive Service were held by women. Jackie Strange became the first female deputy postmaster general in 1985. Strange had started part-time work at the Georgia Teachers College post office in 1946 while she was attending

by about nine miles the distance made by Ruth Law . . . in the fall of 1916," the *Post* continued. She also broke her own record for endurance. Eight days later, when her plane had been repaired, she finished the trip to New York.

Before becoming the first woman to officially transport airmail, Stinson had performed as a stunt pilot at exhibitions. "She looks and smiles like a runaway schoolgirl on a lark and weighs only 103 pounds, but she can slide down a sky bank and do an air loop in a way that makes your hair curl," wrote the *Sunday Telegram* in 1915. In fact, Stinson was the first woman to experimentally carry U.S. mail. As a stunt, she carried mailbags in her plane at the Montana State Fair in 1913 and dropped them at the Helena, Montana, post office.

school there and worked her way up the management ladder. By 2020, forty-one years after Strange got her job, women held 40 percent of senior management positions at USPS.

Megan Brennan was the first woman to be appointed postmaster general, in 2015. She began at USPS in 1986 as a city carrier in Lancaster, Pennsylvania. After several management jobs, she became chief operating officer and executive vice president of USPS in 2010. She retired as postmaster general in 2020. In 2021, 47 percent of postal workers were women, a far cry from the handful who held jobs with the Post Office in the nineteenth century.

ONCE THE EXCEPTION FOR JOBS AS POSTMASTER OR IN OTHER SUPERVISING POSITIONS, WOMEN INCREASINGLY ROSE TO BECOME MANAGERS IN THE POSTAL SERVICE IN THE 1970S AND 1980S. HERE, SENATOR DEBBIE STABENOW (*CENTER*) OF MICHIGAN MEETS WITH HER STATE'S MEMBERS OF THE NATIONAL LEAGUE OF POSTMASTERS. ALL BUT ONE OF THEM ARE WOMEN.

MEGAN BRENNAN STARTED AS A CITY MAIL CARRIER IN PENNSYLVANIA IN THE 1980S. IN 2015, SHE WAS APPOINTED AS THE FIRST FEMALE POSTMASTER GENERAL. HERE SHE DELIVERS A KEYNOTE SPEECH TO CELEBRATE WOMEN'S HISTORY MONTH IN WASHINGTON, DC, IN 2016. BEHIND HER ARE BLOWN-UP PHOTOS OF WOMEN WHO MADE POSTAL HISTORY, INCLUDING BALTIMORE POSTMASTER MARY KATHERINE GODDARD (*LEFT*), AIRMAIL PILOT KATHERINE STINSON (*CENTER*), AND DEPUTY POSTMASTER GENERAL JACKIE STRANGE (*RIGHT*).

8

LATINOS, ASIAN AMERICANS, AND NATIVE AMERICANS IN THE POST OFFICE

L atinos, Asian Americans, and Native Americans combined make up a smaller percentage of postal service workers than African Americans and an even smaller percentage than white workers, both in the past and today. Although the history of African Americans—and of women—in the Post Office is well documented even back to colonial times, there is much less on the record about these other groups. This may be because they came late to the story: many non-white postmasters did not get their jobs until the 1960s, a push that seemed to be helped by the civil rights movement. The majority are concentrated in urban areas. They have also faced widespread discrimination. In the nineteenth century, people of Latino and Asian descent were often seen as foreigners by white workers, although they were born and raised in the United States. This is still sometimes true, even in areas where their communities thrive. Native Americans have a long history of violence and discrimination directed against them.

Latinos come from many countries, including Mexico, the Central and South American nations, and the Caribbean nations. Latinos are Spanish-speaking people of the Americas and also include Portuguese-speaking Brazilians. ("Hispanics" refers to Latinos as well as people who come from Spain. Often the terms "Latinos" and "Hispanics" are used interchangeably in studies.) Asian immigrants also come from many countries, including China, Japan, South Korea, Vietnam, Cambodia, India, Pakistan, Bangladesh, the Philippines, Thailand, Myanmar, Laos, and Indonesia. Native Americans belong to different tribal groups, such as the Sioux, the Navajo, and the Cherokee, whose ancestors lived in what is now the United States prior to the arrival of Europeans.

Although people from these countries or tribal groups differ in culture and language, they are grouped together for national studies. Statistics do not reflect personal identity, but they are a convenient way of measuring overall population information. Though often similar, the stories of Latinos, Asian Americans, and Native Americans in the postal service are unique.

COLONIAL SPAIN HAD A POSTAL SERVICE TO CONNECT MILITARY SETTLEMENTS AND CATHOLIC MISSIONS. THE FIRST CHURCH ON THIS SITE, IN TUMACACORI, ARIZONA, WAS BUILT ON NATIVE AMERICAN LAND IN 1757. THE MISSION SHOWN HERE WAS BUILT IN THE EARLY 1800S AND PHOTOGRAPHED CIRCA 1870.

Latino postal history begins when Florida, California, and the American Southwest were still colonies of Spain. A colonial postal service operated for Spanish Catholic missionaries and soldiers. The United States took over Florida as a territory in 1822 and New Mexico and Arizona in 1850. Texas was annexed in 1844 and became a state in 1845. California became a state in 1850. As soon as these areas

EARLY POSTMASTERS

White people overwhelmingly staffed post offices in Florida, California, and the southwestern states, even where much of the population was Latino. There were exceptions where some Latinos served as postmasters:

★ **John de la Rua** in Pensacola, Florida, in 1831 (He had been the city's mayor.)

★ **Bernardo Segue** in St. Augustine, Florida, in 1831 (He had also been a mayor.)

★ **C. A. Patillo** in Jasper, Texas, in 1847

★ **Augustin Soto** in Laredo, Texas, in 1849

★ **John Francisco** in Rio Arriba, New Mexico, in 1852

★ **Innocencia Martinez** in Taos, New Mexico, in 1853 (She may well have been the first Latina postmaster.)

★ **Refugio Benavides** in Laredo, Texas, from 1859 to 1861 (He was a cattle rancher, mayor, and descendant of Laredo's founder.)

REFUGIO BENAVIDES (*FAR LEFT*) SERVED AS THE POSTMASTER IN LAREDO, TEXAS, FROM 1859 TO 1861. BEFORE THAT, HE WAS THE CITY'S MAYOR. AFTER THE CIVIL WAR BEGAN AND TEXAS SECEDED FROM THE UNION, BENAVIDES BECAME A CONFEDERATE OFFICER. HE IS SHOWN HERE WITH THREE FELLOW CONFEDERATE SOLDIERS FROM LAREDO (*FROM LEFT TO RIGHT*): ATANACIO VIDAURRI, REFUGIO'S BROTHER CRISTOBAL BENAVIDES, AND JOHN Z. LEYENDECKER.

became part of the United States, the Post Office began service. Except, perhaps, in California, where fortune hunters poured in for the gold rush, post offices were few and far between. They multiplied as the West was settled after the Civil War.

Latino postmasters were often influential members of their communities. In 1864, Francisco Ramirez was appointed postmaster of Los Angeles, California. He was a newspaper publisher who frequently wrote editorials about discrimination against Mexican Americans as well as Chinese and African American people living in Los Angeles. In 1869, he became a lawyer, acting as an advocate for these groups.

The U.S. Post Office began mail service in Puerto Rico in 1900, after the United States annexed the country at the close of the Spanish-American War. Puerto Rico became a territory in 1917. One hundred years later, in 2017, it had 118 post offices. Postal staff speak both Spanish and English. After Hurricane Maria devastated the island in 2017, homes and businesses lost electrical power for weeks. But the majority of post offices were able to keep delivering the mail, even to homes that had been damaged and lost all other ways to communicate.

DAMAGE FROM HURRICANE MARIA IN 2017 DESTROYED PUERTO RICO'S ROADS, BUILDINGS, AND INFRASTRUCTURE. USPS BECAME THE MAIN SOURCE OF COMMUNICATION. SINCE ELECTRICAL POWER OUTAGES MADE IT IMPOSSIBLE TO USE CELL PHONES, POSTAL WORKERS ALSO PROVIDED INFORMATION ON THE SICK AND ELDERLY ALONG THEIR ROUTES SO THAT THEY COULD RECEIVE MEDICAL CARE AND DISASTER RELIEF.

USPS has documented some 225 Latinos serving as postmasters in New Mexico and 80 in Texas from 1850 to 1900. There are few records from then until the early 1960s, although some Latinos must have been postal workers in the areas where they lived in great numbers, like California, Texas, New Mexico, Arizona, and Puerto Rico. But this did not mean that they were not discriminated against. In 1912, a Santa Cruz, New Mexico, businessman suggested Ignacio Madrid as the new postmaster. The Post Office replied, "Mr. Madrid . . . can neither read nor write and does not speak English," and turned him down. Decisions were not made based on how many customers would benefit from a postal worker who could speak Spanish.

In 1961, President John F. Kennedy appointed Hector Godinez postmaster of Santa Ana, California. His daughter remembers that "he was one of Kennedy's last appointments—one of four candidates for the job and the only Hispanic. The Santa Ana Chamber [of Commerce] lobbied against his appointment. So did many others. Yet he did become postmaster and he later became president of the Chamber." He rose to become district manager for Southern California, an important administrative job. The post office in Santa Ana was named for him in 2002.

HECTOR GODINEZ (*RIGHT*) BECAME POSTMASTER OF SANTA ANA, CALIFORNIA, IN 1961, UNDER PRESIDENT JOHN F. KENNEDY. HE WAS A CIVIL RIGHTS LEADER IN HIS COMMUNITY. HERE HE WALKS THROUGH A CROWD BESIDE PRESIDENT RICHARD NIXON (*LEFT*), SOMETIME AFTER 1969.

The civil rights movement of the 1960s opened more postal jobs not only to African Americans but all minorities. In 1970, Latino postal workers were active in the wildcat strike for higher wages that began in New York and spread to other cities, disrupting mail processing and delivery for eight days. Hector Gallardo, a Mexican American letter carrier in San Jose, California, was listening to the radio when the music stopped to report a "news flash of the New York City carrier strike. It was like a tidal wave." During local meetings to decide whether to join the strikers, debate was heated, with "people letting off steam." But when they did vote to strike, "everybody was united."

LATINO POSTAL WORKERS OFTEN FACED JOB DISCRIMINATION. HERE, A LARGE GROUP OF LATINOS, INCLUDING MEXICAN AMERICANS, MEET TO PROTEST USPS HIRING PRACTICES IN CHICAGO IN 1978. THEY ARE GATHERED AT THE APARTMENT COMPLEX WHERE CHICAGO'S POSTMASTER LIVED.

Latino postal workers have faced discrimination. One man stated in the late 1990s that "we need more Latino employees and managers because sometimes they discriminate against us if we don't speak proper English, they think we're not smart enough to be supervisors." A supervisor told a Latina worker that she was not dressed properly for work because she looked like she was "going to a fiesta."

In 2003, Latinos made up 7 percent of postal workers. In 2006, USPS made an effort to attract more Latino workers. "It's our goal to continue to look like America, even as the face of America continues to change," Postmaster General John E. Potter told the Hispanic Postal Employee Organization. The population of Latinos in the United States has continued to expand. Between 2010 and 2020, it grew by 23 percent. By 2020, Latinos represented 17 percent of postal workers. Most of these worked in urban centers near where they lived. Suburban and rural post offices tend to be staffed by white Americans. But in cities like Denver, Los Angeles, and San Francisco, where there are many Mexican Americans, Latinos hold a significant number of postal jobs, both in "craft" jobs, like clerks and carriers, and supervisory positions. Chicago, New York, and Philadelphia have many Puerto Rican postal workers. Since a number of Latino clerks and carriers speak Spanish, they can better serve their communities, including those for whom English is a second language. They uphold the mission that the U.S. Postal Service is there for all Americans.

THE OLD POST OFFICE IN HONOLULU, HAWAII, WAS BUILT IN 1869, DURING THE TIME WHEN HAWAII WAS A KINGDOM, NOT A U.S. TERRITORY. THE U.S. POST OFFICE OCCUPIED PART OF THE BUILDING UNTIL 1922. THE ELEGANT BUILDING WAS ONE OF THE BEST-KNOWN AND ADMIRED STRUCTURES OF ITS TIME.

The majority of Asian immigrants and their families have settled in four states: Hawaii, California, New York, and Texas. An early record provides a list of postmasters in Hawaii beginning in 1900. That year, Hawaii became a U.S. territory and U.S. postal service began. Four postmasters of

Asian or Native Hawaiian descent served in towns across the islands. William Hookuanui continued the job he'd held since 1888 as the postmaster at Kaawaihae, on the big island of Hawaii. USPS names sixty Asian or Hawaiian postmasters from 1900 to 1950. Even during World War II, when the United States was at war with Japan, there were postmasters of Japanese descent on the various Hawaiian islands. Although Japanese Americans during the war were interned on the mainland, they were not in Hawaii because they made up a large part of the labor force.

The first large Asian group that came to the United States mainland were Chinese in the 1850s, drawn by the California gold rush and the building of the transcontinental railroad. Until 1965, when the Immigration and Nationality Act became law, immigration laws and laws preventing many Asian immigrants from becoming citizens restricted the number of people who emigrated from Asia. Those who did come faced discrimination in finding jobs, including ones at the Post Office. It is likely that some were hired as postal workers, although this is not well documented. Only several are known to have been postmasters starting in the late 1950s, almost all in the states where Asian American communities were found.

JAPANESE AMERICANS WERE NOT INTERNED ON HAWAII DURING WORLD WAR II BECAUSE THEIR LABOR, MOSTLY AS AGRICULTURAL WORKERS, WAS NEEDED. MANY PEOPLE OF JAPANESE DESCENT WERE INTERNED ON THE U.S. MAINLAND. HERE INTERNEES HELP OUT AT THE POSTAL FACILITY AT THEIR CAMP, SOMETIME BETWEEN 1942 AND 1945.

In 1959, Chu Ching Quong was appointed postmaster of Round Pond, Arkansas. According to USPS, he is the first known Chinese American postmaster in a state other than Hawaii. His sister, Emma Quong Fong, was the first Chinese woman appointed as acting postmaster, in Hughes, Arkansas, from 1956 to 1962.

Lim P. Lee was the first Chinese American to head a major post office, in San Francisco, from 1966 to 1980. He had been a U.S. Army counterintelligence specialist during

World War II and a leading citizen of his city. At that time he was the highest-ranking Chinese American federal appointee. "Lee transformed the face of San Francisco's postal system by increasing the hiring of women, minorities and disabled postal workers," said Congresswoman Nancy Pelosi in 2009, when she asked Congress to name a post office after him. ". . . Mr. Lee worked to ensure while hiring that the post office looked like the rest of the city in terms of its great diversity." Congress named the Chinatown post office in San Francisco in his honor.

CHINATOWN IS A LIVELY NEIGHBORHOOD IN SAN FRANCISCO. LIN POON LEE FOUNDED THE AREA'S BRANCH POST OFFICE IN 1966, THE YEAR HE BECAME THE CITY'S FIRST CHINESE AMERICAN POSTMASTER. THE BUILDING LIES IN THE HEART OF NORTH AMERICA'S OLDEST CHINATOWN. WITH HIS APPOINTMENT, LEE HELD THE HIGHEST FEDERAL JOB OF ANY CHINESE AMERICAN AT THE TIME.

Some Asian Americans feel they were accepted by white supervisors. "I was mentored by [a white] manager . . . [who] asked for help from my supervisor who let me work for the manager on several occasions," explained one worker in an urban mail processing center in the early 2000s. "After the manager saw that I was a good worker, he asked me if I wanted to work with him . . . [W]hen there was an opening in his office he helped me apply for the position, coached me for the interview, and of course, wrote an excellent letter of recommendation for me. I know I am more than qualified for the job but without his help nobody would have known me."

Others have experienced discrimination. An Asian American woman at the same postal facility said, "Sometimes the whites [managers] talk down to me because I am Asian . . . They think because I am Chinese that I don't know what they are saying or something. Like they talk to me like if they are saying, 'Can't you understand English?' I didn't go to college but I was born here and I went to school here so I know exactly what they are saying but they think we all just stepped off the boat."

From 1846 to 2022, there were thirty postmasters and fourteen officers-in-charge in Houston, Texas. Only one postmaster was Asian: Wallace T. Kido, a Japanese American, who served from 1981 to 1983. Joe Singh was an officer-in-charge in 2009. The shortage of Asian American names for management jobs, however, does not mean that Asian Americans are not getting work in the postal service. In 2020, Asian Americans represented 7 percent of the postal labor force. The number rose to 8.3 percent in 2022.

ASIAN AMERICAN FIRSTS

In the twenty-first century, there was a host of first Asian American appointments in California. They started in lower positions in USPS and moved up through the ranks. Manavy Lee, who emigrated from Cambodia at age thirteen, started as a clerk in 1985 in Laguna Beach and in 2008 became the first Asian American postmaster in Lake Forest. In 2012, Ramon C. Sanchez, who started as a part-time mail carrier in 1987, was appointed the first Filipino postmaster in Campbell. Rajinder Sanghera, of Asian Indian descent, was first a mail carrier in San Jose, then became the postmaster of San Francisco in 2012. Avinesh D. Kumar, another Indian American, assumed the job in 2022. Jagdeep K. Grewal, who started out as a window clerk in 1988, was the first Indian American—and woman—to run the post office in Sacramento in 2015.

Between 2000 and 2019, Asian Americans had the fastest population growth rate of all racial and ethnic groups in the United States. Their numbers almost doubled, to 18.9 million people, in 2019. As USPS reflects the diversity of peoples in the country, the number of Asian American postal workers will probably grow with the population.

Native Americans have a different story, since they are not immigrants. They lived on the land that would become the United States for thousands of years prior to the arrival of Europeans. In colonial times, white settlers often used Native peoples to deliver mail for them. These were usually individual runners who might carry only one letter, especially for missionaries or the military. They could navigate through difficult land unfamiliar to white people.

As the 1800s progressed, white American settlers moved to inhabit the midwestern and western parts of the United States. They and the U.S. military pushed Native Americans out of their traditional homelands, usually by force. Native Americans were placed on reservations through treaties that were never fully honored by the federal government. The majority of these reservations were formed in the period from 1850 to 1887. The Yankton Indian

Reservation, for example, occupied by the Sioux, was created in 1858 in the Dakota Territory. The Utes of Colorado ceded much of their land to the federal government in 1874. Although the reservation tribes were partly self-governing, white federal Indian agents had authority to enforce American laws.

NATIVE AMERICANS DID NOT BECOME AMERICAN CITIZENS UNTIL 1924 AND
THEREFORE WERE NOT ELIGIBLE TO BE POSTMASTERS. BUT NINETEENTH-CENTURY
NATIVE AMERICANS DID WORK FOR THE POST OFFICE. THIS 1907 POSTCARD
SHOWS A MAIL CARRIER IN TRADITIONAL DRESS. HE TRANSPORTS THE MAIL
ON A TRAVOIS, A STRUCTURE OF WOODEN POLES THAT DRAGS THE MAILBAG
BEHIND HIS HORSE.

Federal agents—as well as the U.S. Army to stop any resistance—were posted on reservation land. They needed a way to send mail to and from their locations. They needed post offices. But Native American reservations were often placed in remote areas that covered huge distances. The White Mountain reservation for Apache tribes, established in 1872, was as big as the state of Delaware, almost 2,000 square miles. Yet there were only two post offices on the reservation. There were more than a dozen post offices serving white settlers just outside its borders.

But Native Americans frequently used their post offices, especially to reach the government in Washington, DC. They sent hundreds of petitions to the commissioner of Indian Affairs, asking for better food rations and buildings. They also asked for help in keeping white settlers from illegally using their land to graze cattle. They wrote to family and friends who lived on different reservations or to their children, who were forced into government-run boarding schools, which did not allow Native languages to be spoken. Mail also helped them form alliances with different tribes across the country.

Most reservation post offices were run by white federal agents. One exception was Charles Bluejacket, who became the postmaster on a Cherokee Nation reservation in Oklahoma in 1882. At that time, Native peoples were not American citizens. They did not become citizens until 1924. In 1885, the U.S. attorney general decided that "an Indian citizen . . . is not eligible to the office of postmaster." Nevertheless, with reservation post offices so far from Washington, it was a hard rule to enforce. Bluejacket continued to serve as postmaster until 1887, two years after the rule was made.

In the twenty-first century, Native Americans work for USPS both on and off reservations. Navajo Steve Begay, a former U.S. Marine, worked in Phoenix, Arizona, as a mail carrier for six years. In 2013, he was appointed postmaster of the Farmington post office on the Arizona reservation. Native Americans were already serving as postmasters in Gallup, New Mexico, and Window Rock, Arizona. But in 2021, Native Americans and Alaskan Natives made up less than 2 percent of the postal workforce, including those who do not work on reservations.

Post offices on reservations are still few and far between. "Many homes on reservations do not have addresses or have 'non-traditional addresses' that do not use a street name. The postal service does not deliver to these addresses," according to the Native American Rights Fund (NARF). Therefore, many Native Americans have post office boxes, but they need to travel to reach them. Post office boxes are numbered cubicles that are housed in the post offices themselves and are typically locked, with the user having a key. They hold mail and packages until they are picked up by the owners,

THIS VIEW OF THE HIGHWAY THROUGH THE CHEYENNE RIVER SIOUX RESERVATION SHOWS HOW EMPTY OF HOMES AND BUSINESSES THE RESERVATION IS FOR MILES AROUND. POST OFFICES ARE FEW AND FAR BETWEEN.

who pay a fee to have the boxes. "[S]ome Navajo members travel 140 miles roundtrip to access postal services," NARF continued. "Some Fort Peck members in Montana travel 34 miles each way."

When small post offices close because they do not have enough customers by USPS standards, those on reservations are vulnerable. This has been a hardship for people who depend on the mail for medicine, Social Security checks, or packages from friends or family in other places. Decisions about policy and location affect not only postal

RICO LANÁAT' WORL, A TLINGIT/ATHABASCAN ARTIST BASED IN ALASKA, SHOWS HIS ART, *RAVEN STORY*, WHICH HE CREATED FOR A NORTHWEST COAST ART STAMP.

employees but the people they serve. For Native Americans, and for Latinos and Asians for whom English is a second language, a multilingual staff gives them better access to services most Americans take for granted. It is also a benefit for USPS, which prides itself on hiring a more diverse workforce than almost any other business in the United States.

9

U.S. POSTAL INSPECTION SERVICE

n June 1871, the *New York Times* listed some of the wonderful things for sale in circulars sent through the mail. They promised information on "how to cure hysterics and lockjaw; . . . how to make diamonds at small expense; . . . how to live a hundred years; how to kill rats; how to make artificial money; how to curl hair." Also advertised was "THE MAGIC BELT! FOR RENDERING ONE'S SELF 'INVISIBLE.'" The circular went on to explain, "To become invisible, buckle it around your waist; . . . Go where you will, no living being can see you, nor in any way be aware of your presence."

To acquire any of these items, one only had to send money through the mail to the advertiser. One might or might not receive some version of the product advertised.

THIS AD PROMISES "A SURE CURE" FOR "ALL BRAIN WORKERS, IN EVERY CAPACITY OF LIFE" BY WEARING "HILL'S GENUINE MAGNETIC ANTI-HEADACHE CAP." CUSTOMERS COULD MAIL IN $3.00 AND MIGHT OR MIGHT NOT RECEIVE A CAP IN RETURN. FRAUDULENT CLAIMS LIKE THIS WERE COMMON IN THE LATE NINETEENTH CENTURY.

A BOON FOR ALL BRAIN WORKERS.

For Nervous Headaches, for Impaired Eyesight, for Railway Passengers, Editors, Lawyers, Professors, Authors, Merchants, Book-keepers, Business Men, Business Ladies, Architects, Active Salesmen, and all Brain Workers, in Every Capacity of Life, will find, upon trial, that

Hill's Genuine Magnetic Anti-Headache Cap
Is a Brain-food Unequalled in the Known World. It

furnishes and supplies Nature's demands, viz., Magnetism, which moves the blood in our veins, the muscles and the nerves of our bodies.

These caps are made of silk and contain twenty-two (22) of Hill's Grand Medal Magnetic Storage Batteries, polarized and scientifically arranged, so that each will furnish positive and negative currents of pure Magnetism to the brain, flesh and blood. They never produce shocks or sores like "Electric" devices, but always soothe, strengthen and invigorate. They furnish Nature's remedy for insomnia. The superior curative powers of Hill's Magnetic Appliances are well known throughout the land, with bushels of testimonials for such as desire. The price of this cap is only $3.00. Will be mailed to any address in the U.S., with postage prepaid, on receipt of the price, in M.O. or registered letter. Give size of hat worn, and address

HILL MAGNETIC APPLIANCE CO.,
READING, MASS.

"The largest business in the swindling circular line is that of advertising for sale counterfeit money," the *Times* article continued. "The mail-bags are literally flooded with those circulars." In return for a "small" amount of money, the purchaser would receive counterfeit bills of greater value. "It is this using the public mails with impunity to educate the country to crime, which is the most serious phase of the whole matter. These circulars go to all classes of people; they are addressed to every individual whose name and post-office can be copied from directories, from the advertisements and reports of meetings in country papers, and from the registers in hotels."

It was, and is, the job of the United States Postal Inspection Service (USPIS) to track down the creators of these fraudulent offers and put a stop to them. USPIS often works in cooperation with other federal agencies, like the FBI. It is arguably the oldest federal law enforcement agency in the United States. In August 1775, the new American government appointed a "surveyor" to make sure there was no dishonesty in the operations of post offices. Starting in 1801, these surveyors were called "special agents." Their job included investigating mail robberies. In the 1820s, in addition to investigating "cases of mail robberies and of missing letters," agents were to keep an eye on "the characters and conduct of postmasters."

With swindles frequently being carried out through the mail, in 1872 Congress passed the first act against mail fraud. The act made it a crime to use the U.S. Post Office (or a private delivery service) to carry out "any scheme or artifice to defraud, or for obtaining money or property by means of false or fraudulent pretenses, representations, or promises."

Postal inspectors also went after fraudulent lottery schemes. A lottery is a way to raise money by selling tickets to many people. When the winning ticket is drawn, the person holding it usually receives a big cash prize. In the nineteenth century, fake lotteries were advertised in the mail. People sent in their money for tickets. But there was no drawing or cash prize. The Anti-Lottery Act of 1890 made it illegal to use the mail to sell lottery tickets.

POSTAL INSPECTOR JOHN CHUM TRAVELS THROUGH ALASKA, CHECKING ON POSTAL FACILITIES, CIRCA 1898. ONE OF THE EARLY JOBS OF WHAT BECAME THE POSTAL INSPECTION SERVICE WAS TO MAKE SURE THAT "THE CHARACTERS AND CONDUCT OF POSTMASTERS" UPHELD THE STANDARDS OF THE POST OFFICE.

In 1920, Charles Ponzi offered Americans the chance to make a 50 percent profit in forty-five days by giving him money to buy and resell return postage coupons. He paid the first round of investors back with funds given by the second round of investors. He paid the second round with funds given by the third round of investors, and so on. Ponzi never actually bought or sold any coupons. This is called a pyramid

scheme, because a small number of first-time investors are unwittingly being supported by more and more investors underneath them. It goes on until there are no more new investors—and no money to pay all except the top rungs back. Tens of thousands of investors believed him. Ponzi made about $15 million in eight months until his scheme was uncovered. Since he was using the mail to

CHARLES PONZI, SHOWN HERE IN 1920, CARRIED OUT ONE OF THE MOST FAMOUS FRAUDS IN AMERICAN HISTORY. HE PROMISED INVESTORS A 50-PERCENT PROFIT IN A SCHEME TO RESELL FOREIGN POSTAGE COUPONS. HE THEN USED THE MONEY FROM EACH GROUP OF INVESTORS TO PAY OFF THE ONE ABOVE IT, UNTIL THE NUMBER OF INVESTORS—AND THE MONEY—RAN OUT. HE NEVER ACTUALLY INTENDED TO PAY EVERYONE.

send letters to his investors, postal inspectors were part of the investigative team that put a stop to the fraud. He served three and a half years of a five-year prison sentence.

Another of the USPIS's jobs is to track down and apprehend people who actually steal the mail. Since 1855, the Post Office has transported valuables by registered mail, including gold, cash, bonds, and jewelry. Registered mail must be signed for by the recipient to make sure it gets delivered to the right person. Carrying valuables makes Post Office vehicles and buildings a tempting target for criminals. On June 2, 1899, members of the Hole in the Wall gang—the group of outlaws assembled by Butch Cassidy (Robert LeRoy Parker) and joined by the Sundance Kid (Harry Longabaugh)—held up the mail and express cars of the Union Pacific Railroad.

ROBERT LEROY PARKER, BETTER KNOWN AS BUTCH CASSIDY (FRONT ROW, RIGHT) IS SHOWN HERE WITH MEMBERS OF THE WILD BUNCH OR HOLE IN THE WALL GANG: HARRY A. LONGABAUGH (THE SUNDANCE KID, FRONT ROW LEFT), BEN KILPATRICK (FRONT ROW, CENTER),WILL CARVER (STANDING, LEFT), AND HARVEY LOGAN (STANDING, RIGHT). IN 1899, THE GANG HELD UP A TRAIN IN WYOMING, BLOWING UP THE MAIL CAR AND ESCAPING WITH A FORTUNE IN BANKNOTES AND GOLD.

GETTING AWAY
WITH MONEY

The postal workers who were held up by the Hole in the Wall gang lived to tell the tale. "The robbers mounted the [train] engine and at the point of their guns forced the engineer and fireman to dismount . . . and marched them over to our car," eyewitness and mail clerk Robert Lawson told the *Buffalo (Wyoming) Bulletin*.

". . . Burt Bruce, clerk in charge, refused to open the door . . . There was much loud talk and threats to blow up the car . . . In about 15 minutes two shots were fired into the car . . .

The Newton Boys—four brothers from Texas—and their partners in crime were apprehended soon after they robbed the mail car on the Chicago, Milwaukee, and St. Paul Railway on June 12, 1924. Two of the brothers secretly boarded the train in Chicago. They climbed into the engine car and forced the engineer to stop the train at a remote point on the route. They took more than $3 million from the mail car, the largest train robbery in history. Unfortunately for the brothers, one of them was shot five times by a coconspirator who thought he was a postal clerk in the confusion. He was taken to Chicago, where a doctor turned the brothers in. All four

"Following close behind the shooting came a terrific explosion, and one of the doors was completely wrecked and most of the car windows broken . . .

"The robbers then went after the safes in the express car with dynamite and soon succeeded in getting into them, but not before the car was torn to pieces."

The gang escaped with an estimated $30,000 worth of banknotes and goods (over $1.1 million in today's money). They were not apprehended for this robbery. Butch Cassidy and the Sundance Kid were thought to be killed in South America in 1908.

of them served prison sentences.

In 1933, members of the gang of Roger "the Terrible" Touhy, a Chicago gangster, stopped a mail truck in Charlotte, North

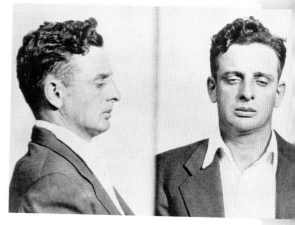

THIS 1933 POLICE MUG SHOT SHOWS ROGER "THE TERRIBLE" TOUHY, A GANGSTER BASED IN CHICAGO. THE SAME YEAR, MEMBERS OF HIS GANG ROBBED A MAIL TRUCK AND POST OFFICE IN CHARLOTTE, NORTH CAROLINA. THREE OF THEM WERE QUICKLY CAUGHT AND SERVED TIME IN JAIL.

Carolina, by driving out in front of it. At least one of the gang members carried a machine gun. They disarmed the truck driver and used wire cutters to clip through the lock on the

RELIABLE ENOUGH TO TRANSPORT A DIAMOND

How do you securely send perhaps the world's most famous diamond from New York City to Washington, DC? Owner and jeweler Harry Winston sent it through the U.S. mail. "It's the safest way to mail gems," Winston explained. "I've sent gems all over the world that way."

When Winston donated the Hope Diamond to the Smithsonian Institution, he needed it delivered from his office to the Museum of Natural History. The 45.52-carat blue diamond—blue diamonds are especially rare—was sent registered mail on November 8, 1958. The postage was $2.44. Winston also paid an additional $142.85 for $1 million insurance in case the package was lost. The diamond was wrapped in plain brown paper and addressed simply to "Smithsonian Institution, Washington, D.C."

On November 10, postal carrier James G. Todd transported the diamond from the DC post office to the museum in a regular mailbag. Secretary of the Smithsonian Leonard Carmichael received it. The Post Office's job was complete.

truck. Inside, they found a mail clerk and about $100,000 in cash and banknotes. They took the money and left the clerk. Two weeks after the theft, most of the robbers were in jail.

The Hope Diamond, brought from India to France in the seventeenth century, had passed through the hands of several owners. The owners were rumored to be cursed with misfortune. Within a year after delivering the diamond, postal carrier Todd was injured in two car accidents, his wife and dog died, and his home was partially destroyed in a fire. Asked about the curse, Todd said, "I don't believe any of that stuff. . . If the hex is supposed to affect the owners, then the public should be having the bad luck."

The Smithsonian is a public institution partly funded by the U.S. government.

IN 1958, JEWELER HARRY WINSTON PAID $2.44 IN POSTAGE—PLUS $142.85 FOR $1 MILLION WORTH OF INSURANCE—TO HAVE THE HOPE DIAMOND SENT FROM NEW YORK TO THE SMITHSONIAN INSTITUTION IN WASHINGTON, DC. THE ORIGINAL WRAPPER, COVERED WITH SEVENTEEN STRIPS OF METERED POSTAGE, WAS MARKED "PLEASE DELIVER 11:45 AM 11/10/58." LETTER CARRIER JAMES TODD MADE THE DELIVERY ON TIME.

Mail train robberies were common enough that in 1921 the Post Office armed railway mail clerks with surplus Army World War I revolvers. These were replaced by .38-caliber revolvers in 1930. Kenneth Race, a railway clerk in the 1950s, remembered, "At the end of our run, if we got any Registered Mail they would hand you the sack and a gun so you could guard it while you took it to the Postmaster. I was never sure that I would want to have a gun fight over that bag of mail but luckily I never had to make that decision."

U. S. Gold Depository, Ft. Knox, Ky.

69810

THIS VINTAGE POSTCARD, CIRCA 1930–1945, SHOWS THE U.S. GOLD DEPOSITORY AT FT. KNOX, KENTUCKY. GOLD WAS SHIPPED THERE FROM PHILADELPHIA AND NEW YORK BY REGISTERED MAIL. THE POSTAL INSPECTION SERVICE BOTH MANAGED THE EFFORT AND PROVIDED SECURITY WITH OTHER LOCAL AND FEDERAL OFFICIALS AND THE U.S. TREASURY DEPARTMENT.

Postal inspectors, with other federal agents, have also been responsible for seeing that large shipments of gold are safely transported. In 1892, they supervised the mailing of $20 million in gold from California to Washington, DC. In 1937, the first shipment of gold to the newly opened Fort Knox Bullion Depository in Kentucky came by mail train from the Philadelphia Mint and the New York Assay Office.

USPIS tackles a range of other crimes and criminals. It goes after credit card theft—millions of credit cards are sent by banks through the mail—and identity theft. Postal inspectors track down thieves who pull bills and other financial documents from the mail to gather enough information to assume a person's identity. They also track down senders of illegal drugs and intercept payments for drugs that are mailed. They continue to apprehend the perpetrators of mail fraud schemes.

Interestingly, women were slower to get jobs in USPIS than in other areas of the postal service. The first two, Janene Gordon and Jane Currie, were not hired until 1971. Gordon was told to "show up with [her] hat and tie" for her interview. She did not, but she got the job. In the 1970s, when a phone call reporting a postal crime was put through to her, most of the callers said, "No, I want to talk to a real inspector."

NOTABLE ARRESTS

★ **Ivan Boesky** and **Michael Milken**, for insider trading—using information the public did not get in order to make money for themselves in the stock market, 1987

★ Televangelist **Jim Bakker**, for receiving $178 million from viewers who thought they were contributing to the development of a Christian theme park, 1989

★ **Leon Amiel**, for leading a billion-dollar art forgery ring, 1991 (Forgeries of art sent through the mail included works by Pablo Picasso, Marc Chagall, Salvador Dalí, and Joan Miró.)

★ **Ted Kaczynski**, the "Unabomber," whose mail bombs killed three people and injured others (After a seventeen-year search, he was arrested in 1996.)

★ **Ralph Esmerian**, owner of a luxury jewelry company, charged with fraud and embezzlement, 2010

★ **Stephen Bannon**, former assistant to President Donald Trump, arrested on a friend's yacht for a fraudulent scheme to raise money for a "non-government project" to build a wall between the United States and Mexico. Brian Kolfage, Andrew Badolato, and Timothy Shea, who participated in the scheme, were also indicted. Bannon was pardoned for committing a federal crime by President Trump in 2021 before he ever went to trial. Kolfage and Badolato pled guilty without a trial in spring 2022. Shea's June 2022 trial was declared a mistrial—a hung jury could not agree on whether he was guilty or not guilty.

Nevertheless, she did not retire until 2004; by then, many women had joined the service. Now they work side by side with men.

In 2020, postal inspectors made nearly 5,000 arrests involving postal crimes. These included mail theft, mail fraud, and prohibited mailings. More than 3,500 of those arrested were convicted. "It doesn't matter what the mail piece is. A greeting card from Aunt Minnie. A multimillion-dollar credit card promotion . . . [A]ll postal customers are guaranteed equal access to the agency's formidable investigative powers," read a USPS official publication in 2009. "And," it added, "it's all included in the price of postage!"

10 THE POST OFFICE OF THE FUTURE

n 2006, Congress passed the Postal Accountability and Enhancement Act (PAEA) in order to attempt to fix USPS's continual financial problems. The law gave USPS greater ability to raise postage charges on its own. It mandated that USPS continue to deliver mail six days a week, including Saturday. But many government leaders, the press, historians, and postal unions believed that the PAEA created as many or even more problems for USPS as it solved.

Attempts to raise or lower postage rates were still overseen by the Postal Regulatory Commission. Since the commission's five members are appointed by the president, the political party the president belongs to can still influence its decisions. USPS itself does not have the authority to work

PRESIDENT GEORGE W. BUSH SIGNS THE 2006 POSTAL ACCOUNTABILITY AND
ENHANCEMENT ACT (PAEA) INTO LAW, WITH MEMBERS OF CONGRESS LOOKING ON.
MEANT TO IMPROVE THE POSTAL SERVICE, THE LAW REQUIRED USPS TO PREPAY
HEALTH CARE BENEFITS DECADES BEFORE EMPLOYEES RETIRED, PLACING AN
ENORMOUS FINANCIAL BURDEN ON THE SERVICE THAT IT COULD NOT MEET.

as an independent business. Although Saturday delivery
is popular, it involves more workers and costs more money
than just delivering mail five days a week.

The law confirmed that USPS could only deliver letters,
packages, and printed matter like magazines and catalogs.
It was not allowed to experiment with offering electronic
services that could make it more competitive with private

delivery services. And USPS was required to prepay the estimated cost of health care benefits for its workers fifty years in advance.

This was the most devastating requirement for USPS. In addition to all its other operating costs, the service was obligated to pay more than $5 billion each year into a pension health fund that workers would not touch for decades. The reason Congress called for this payment was that it was afraid the postal service would go bankrupt in the future and the government would be left to bail it out. If the money for health benefits was there ahead of time, there would be no need for Congress to provide it. No other federal agency or any business is required to do this. The pre-funding requirement all but guaranteed that USPS would operate at a great loss every year.

USPS managed to make several payments until 2011. Congress did nothing to actually force USPS to comply with the law. It continued recording deficits. In 2020, it lost $9.2 billion.

In 2020, USPS was faced with another crisis: how to process and deliver mail while the country was under lockdown to prevent the coronavirus from spreading. Because of the COVID-19 pandemic, businesses were sending significantly less marketing and advertising mail, a source of USPS income. Personal mail declined too. USPS was selling fewer stamps and fewer people were using more expensive services like Priority Mail Express. Thousands of workers who caught the virus were not there to do their jobs. Delivery time slowed. Although some mail arrived when expected, it took longer for USPS to process the mail coming in and to deliver it.

During the COVID-19 pandemic, however, the number of packages increased. Stuck at home, Americans were buying online and having their goods delivered to them. In a Harris Poll released in June 2020, more than 2,000 Americans were asked what companies they considered essential to fill their needs during this time. USPS received the majority of votes, coming in first.

ALTHOUGH THE COVID-19 PANDEMIC HIT USPS HARD IN 2020, IT ROSE TO THE CHALLENGE WHEN IT DELIVERED FREE HOME COVID TESTS TO ANY AMERICAN WHO REQUESTED ONE. IN JANUARY AND FEBRUARY 2022 ALONE IT DELIVERED MORE THAN 68 MILLION PACKAGES, WITH FOUR TESTS TO A KIT.

Package delivery helped bring in needed income. In fact, because USPS has such a vast network of delivery routes, private companies like FedEx and UPS pay USPS to deliver hundreds of millions of packages. These private companies deliver in heavily populated areas. They are not interested in going to remote places. FedEx and UPS packages go to a major postal center. Then USPS carriers deliver them for what is called the "last mile": the effort it takes to get a package to its final home or business destination. But even this income was not enough to offset the postal service deficit.

With the COVID-19 pandemic raging, USPS faced another problem as the presidential election in November approached. Then Republican president Donald Trump and Democrat Joe Biden were running for the office. It was clear that many people would send in their voting ballots by mail, since voting in person was a risk for catching the virus. Votes that are mailed in are just as legal and acceptable as those cast in person. Some Americans, including President Trump, believed that more Democrats than Republicans would choose to vote by mail. Trump alarmed the public by stating in a news briefing and a follow-up broadcast interview that USPS could never handle the millions of ballots that would be cast, although he offered no proof. If ballots were not delivered in time, they could not be counted.

A WOMAN PLACES HER MAIL-IN VOTING BALLOT INTO A MAILBOX IN CALIFORNIA IN SEPTEMBER 2020. VOTING BY MAIL BECAME AN ISSUE IN THE 2020 ELECTION FOR PRESIDENT BETWEEN DONALD TRUMP AND JOE BIDEN, WHEN PRESIDENT TRUMP QUESTIONED THE VALIDITY OF MAIL-IN BALLOTS AND REFUSED EXTRA FUNDING FOR USPS TO ENSURE THAT THEY WOULD BE DELIVERED ON TIME.

"They don't have the money to do the universal mail-in voting. So therefore they can't do it, I guess," Trump declared in August. He refused to sign legislation that would have given USPS more funds.

"Now, they need that money in order to make the Post Office work, so it can take all of these millions and millions of ballots," he continued. "Now, if we [the Trump administration] don't make a deal [with Congress], that means they don't get the money. That means they can't have universal mail-in voting, they just can't have it." By refusing to allow Congress to pass emergency funding, Trump was almost ensuring USPS would fail.

At the same time, Louis DeJoy, the postmaster general, announced cuts to postal service. Two federal judges ordered USPS to deliver all mail, even if this meant operating later-than-normal hours and adding extra mail collections. The judges wanted to be sure that mail-in ballots would not be delayed so that they could be counted. USPS succeeded in delivering most ballots on time. Joe Biden won the presidential election.

DEMONSTRATORS IN RENO, NEVADA, PROTEST THE LIMITING OF MAIL SERVICES BEFORE THE 2020 PRESIDENTIAL ELECTION. MANY AMERICANS FEARED THEIR BALLOTS WOULD NOT BE DELIVERED IN TIME TO BE COUNTED. THE POSSIBILITY WAS ESPECIALLY TRUE FOR RURAL AMERICANS, WHO OFTEN LIVE FARTHER AWAY FROM A POST OFFICE AND HAVE SLOWER MAIL DELIVERY THAN THOSE LIVING IN CITIES.

MAIL-IN BALLOTING ON AMERICAN INDIAN RESERVATIONS

USPS operates post offices on American Indian reservations, but they are few and far between. These post offices operate for limited hours. Therefore, it is difficult for people on reservations to both receive a mail-in ballot and deliver it to the post office nearest to them in time to be counted. Late ballots are not counted.

The 2020 election made this issue clear on reservations throughout the country. It highlights a larger problem faced by other rural Americans as well. Solutions have been suggested. They include using mobile and temporary voting stations during election time, allowing people to both register for voting and vote at these stations on the same day, and increasing the number of ballot drop-off boxes so that no one needs to travel more than twenty miles to reach one. The Postal Service Reform Act of 2022 did not deal with this issue.

In October 2021, Postmaster General DeJoy's ten-year strategic plan for overhauling USPS, called "Delivering for America," went into effect. While for decades First-Class Mail took no longer than three days to deliver, under the new plan it can take up to five days. One reason is that while

USPS used to send 20 percent of First-Class Mail by air, it now sends only 12 percent. The rest is transported by truck. USPS stated that 61 percent of First-Class Mail would not be affected. That means 39 percent—not a small number—would take longer to reach their destinations.

Only months later, in March 2022, Congress finally passed the Postal Service Reform Act, the first such act since 2006. President Joe Biden signed it into law on April 6. It canceled the debt USPS owed for not paying its health care benefits years ahead of time. It provides more funds to run USPS. But it does not tell the postal service how to use these funds.

MEMBERS OF CONGRESS APPLAUD AFTER PRESIDENT JOE BIDEN SIGNS THE 2022 POSTAL SERVICE REFORM ACT INTO LAW ON APRIL 6. THE LAW RELIEVED USPS OF ITS DEBT AND PROVIDED MUCH-NEEDED FUNDING TO KEEP THE SERVICE RUNNING.

WHAT THE POSTAL SERVICE REFORM ACT OF 2022 CALLS FOR

★ Mail will continue to be delivered six days a week everywhere in the United States.

★ USPS can modernize postal facilities and equipment.

★ When USPS workers retire, they will go on the Medicare plan, open to all Americans sixty-five and over, instead of the traditional postal service health care plan, saving billions of dollars.

★ USPS will be able to offload services they now provide to state, local, and tribal governments, including issuing passports, hunting, and fishing licenses.

★ USPS workers will get updated technology for more reliable tracking information on where a piece of mail is at any time.

The current postmaster general can make the changes he wishes, for good or bad. Any new postmaster general will also have this ability to set policy, to keep things as is or make alterations.

The Postal Service Reform Act is a compromise. Democrats and Republicans both had to give up provisions they wanted so it would pass. "Our country is pretty divided right now, let's be honest," said Ohio senator Rob Portman, who cosponsored the bill. "But one enduring reality about our country is that we have a post office that ties us all together, and everybody depends on that post office."

WHAT THE ACT DOES NOT DO

★ Small post offices can still be closed completely or have limited counter service hours.

★ Postage charges will not be lowered. Stamp prices will still keep rising.

★ No provisions protect mail-in voting.

★ The act does not require USPS to be totally self-supporting financially.

EPILOGUE

The Postal Service Reform Act of 2022 raises hopes that USPS will stay in business. "Do we really want to ditch this 246-year-old institution . . . because what's trending downward is personal correspondence?" said Philip Rubio in a 2021 interview. Rubio is a prominent professor of postal labor history. He was also a postal worker himself for many years. "The Post Office . . . in the past, [has] been able to influence trends and also innovate and adapt." He believes it can continue to do so.

THE NATIONAL POSTAL MUSEUM IN WASHINGTON, DC, DRAWS VISITORS FROM AROUND THE WORLD TO SEE ITS VAST COLLECTION OF STAMPS AND EXHIBITS LIKE THE ONES IN THIS PHOTO, REVEALING A TREASURE TROVE OF POSTAL MEMORABILIA. THE MUSEUM OPENED IN 1993 AND IS HOUSED IN WHAT WAS THE CITY POST OFFICE BUILDING.

Suggestions have been made to improve USPS's ability to make more money beyond what is in the 2022 law. One of these is to let it offer electronic services. Post offices could provide free Wi-Fi access and make computers and printers available to the public. Another option is to provide financial services to consumers at post offices. About 66 million Americans in 2020 did not have a bank account at all or banked a small amount of money that hardly covered banking costs.

In 2020, a bill to bring back postal banking was introduced in Congress. It would offer "low-cost checking and savings accounts, ATMs, mobile banking, and low-interest loans," according to a press release from the office of Senator Kirsten Gillibrand, one of its sponsors. "The USPS is the only institution that serves every community in the country . . . ," Gillibrand said. "The *Postal Banking Act* would . . . establish postal banking for the nearly 10 million American households who lack access to basic financial services." Even after postal savings banks ended in 1966, USPS has continued to offer one vital financial service. It issues money orders—more than $20 billion worth a year. Money orders have helped millions of Americans who are not served by commercial banks to send money to businesses and families.

Many Americans feel emotional about the Post Office.

The local post office has been a meeting place and community center for more than two centuries. People picking up their mail or dropping off letters and packages chat and exchange news and family stories. Postal workers, both window clerks and letter carriers, have regular contact with the people they serve. They are their neighbors and friends. For many Americans, the postal system has been the only daily contact they have with a federal agency. In survey after survey it ranks as the most popular government agency.

THE NATIONAL POSTAL MUSEUM'S INSTALLATION "WINDOWS INTO AMERICA" REPRODUCES THE IMAGES OF FIFTY-FOUR STAMPS FROM OVER FOUR THOUSAND IN THE MUSEUM'S COLLECTION. IT IS A GLOWING TRIBUTE TO WHAT MAIL SERVICE HAS CONTRIBUTED TO THE UNITED STATES.

"[The] post office . . . is one of the last threads of universal community, it's a service that we share in this country," said one of several Americans on a WNYC public radio podcast in 2021 about support for USPS. "I can count on communicating with someone this way more reliably than any other. This is one essential social and community glue that I really, really value and would hate to see it go . . . We talk about improving communities. [It] is already here."

Perhaps the strongest reason for keeping USPS as a public service isn't nostalgia but that, for all its flaws, it does the best job of reaching out to all Americans at a reasonable cost. Even technology like email and rising labor costs cannot change the fact that USPS has the best transportation and communication network already in place in the United States. This is not only a testament to the U.S. Postal Service's past history but a measure of its value in the future.

TIMELINE

1753 ★ The British government appoints Benjamin Franklin as the deputy postmaster general of its colonies.

1772 ★ Benjamin Franklin creates the job of "surveyor" to regulate post offices and investigate thefts; this is the beginning of the U.S. Postal Inspection Service.

1775 ★ The Continental Congress appoints Benjamin Franklin as postmaster general for the new United States.

★ Mary Katherine Goddard is considered the first American woman to serve as a postmaster, in Baltimore.

1788 ★ The new U.S. Constitution mandates a postal service in article 1, section 8.

1792 ★ Congress passes the Post Office Act, establishing postal routes.

1802 ★ Congress passes a law allowing only "free white person[s]" to carry the mail. The law stays in place until 1865.

1823 ★ Congress declares waterways are postal routes.

1825 ★ The Dead Letter Office for undeliverable mail opens.

1829 ★ The office of postmaster general becomes part of the president's cabinet.

1831 ★ John de la Rua is the first known Latino postmaster, serving in Pensacola, Florida.

1835 ★ Abolitionist literature is sent by mail to South Carolina, where it is burned by white residents of Charleston.

1838 ★ Congress declares railroads are postal routes.

1845 ★ Congress passes an act that establishes Star Routes.

1847 ★ The first printed U.S. postal stamps are issued.

1848 ★ The California gold rush begins. Mail is transported by steamboat from the East and West Coasts, crossing by land the Isthmus of Panama.

1850 TO 1870 ★ The majority of Native American reservations are formed. Post offices are few and far between, located to serve the U.S. Army and white employees of the Bureau of Indian Affairs.

1855 ★ All postage must be prepaid by the sender using stamps.

★ Registered mail begins.

1860 ★ The Pony Express begins; it ends in 1861.

1861 ★ The Civil War between the Union and Confederate States begins; it ends in 1865.

1862 ★ William Cooper Nell is the first known African American appointed as a clerk, in the Boston post office.

1863 ★ Free city delivery begins.

1864 ★ Railway Mail Service officially begins; it ends in 1977.

★ The first money orders for use in the United States are sold.

1865 ★ For the first time, female clerks in the Post Office headquarters' Dead Letter Office outnumber male clerks.

1867 ★ The L. F. Ward Company invents the mail crane, used to move mailbags to and from trains and platforms.

1872 ★ Congress passes the first mail fraud statute.

1882 ★ Charles Bluejacket becomes postmaster on a Cherokee Nation reservation. The U.S. attorney general decides that since Native Americans are not American citizens (until 1924), they cannot serve as postal workers.

A YOUNG BOY REACHES TO DEPOSIT HIS LETTERS IN A POST OFFICE MAILBOX, CIRCA 1880.

1883 ★ The Civil Service Act requires that applicants for federal positions, including those in the Post Office, take an exam to qualify. This allows more African Americans to be hired.

1893 ★ The first commemorative stamps are issued.

1896 ★ Rural Free Delivery starts as an experiment; it becomes a permanent service in 1902.

1899 ★ The first women are hired as carriers on rural routes; the first woman city carrier is not hired until 1917.

1900 ★ U.S. mail service starts in Puerto Rico, even before it becomes a U.S. territory in 1917.

　　　 ★ Hawaii becomes a U.S. territory and mail service begins. Many of the first postmasters are of Asian or Native Hawaiian descent.

A POSTAL WORKER STANDS NEXT TO HIS THREE-WHEELED MOTORCYCLE IN 1912. MOTORCYCLES WERE USED TO TRANSPORT MAIL INTO THE 1920S.

1911 ★ Postal banking system begins; it ends in 1966.

1913 ★ Parcel post begins.

★ Postmaster General Albert Burleson, appointed by President Woodrow Wilson, segregates Black and white postal workers. Some Black postal workers lose their jobs or are demoted.

★ The National Alliance of Postal and Federal Employees, organized by African American railway mail clerks, is formed to resist discrimination.

1914 ★ The Post Office begins its motorized vehicle service; it owns and operates trucks and other ground vehicles.

1918 ★ Scheduled airmail service begins.

1920 ★ The U.S. Postal Inspection Service uncovers Charles Ponzi's fraudulent investment scheme.

HORSES AND WAGONS WERE STILL DELIVERING MAIL IN 1913, WHEN THIS PHOTO WAS TAKEN.

1923 ★ Mailboxes or mail slots in doors are required for home city delivery.

1925 ★ Congress passes an act that allows the Post Office to contract for airmail service from commercial airlines.

1937 ★ The Postal Inspection Service begins the transfer of the U.S. gold reserve from New York to Fort Knox, Kentucky; the gold is sent by registered mail.

1941 ★ Highway Post Offices begin; they end in 1974.

      ★ The United States enters World War II after Japan bombs Pearl Harbor in Hawaii.

1942 ★ The Post Office begins V-mail; the last V-mail is sent in 1945, at the close of World War II.

      ★ Immigrants and Americans of Japanese descent, primarily living on the West Coast, are interned in remote camps. The last camp closes in 1946.

1943 ★ Postal zoning system is put in place in large cities.

1958 ★ The Hope Diamond is sent from New York to the Smithsonian Institution in Washington, DC, by mail.

1959 ★ Chu Ching Quong is the first known Chinese American man to be appointed postmaster, in Round Pond, Arkansas.

1961 ★ Christopher C. Scott becomes assistant postmaster general for transportation, the highest position ever held by an African American in the postal service.

1963 ★ Zip codes with five numbers are introduced; zip codes with four additional numbers are introduced in 1983.

1966 ★ The main post office in Chicago shuts down for ten days, overwhelmed by the volume of mail it has to handle.

1968 ★ The category of Priority Mail is established.

1970 ★ Letter carriers in New York City begin a wildcat strike for better pay that spreads to post offices across the country.

★ The Postal Reorganization Act is signed by President Richard Nixon into law.

★ The category of Express Mail (changed to "Priority Mail Express" in 2013) is established as an experiment; it becomes permanent in 1977.

1971 ★ United States Postal Service (USPS) begins.

★ The board of governors, not the president, now appoints postmaster general.

★ For the first time, a postal labor contract is negotiated

through collective bargaining between the federal government and the postal unions.

1977 ★ Airmail is no longer a special service that costs more; all long-distance mail in the United States goes by air.

1982 ★ The first use of automation in post offices begins with optical character readers.

1993 ★ The National Postal Museum opens in Washington, DC; it is a branch of the Smithsonian Institution.

A YOUNG GIRL DEPOSITS A LETTER IN A MAILBOX IN 1920. THE SHAPE AND SIZE OF POST OFFICE MAILBOXES IMPROVED OVER TIME SO THAT THEY WOULD BE EASIER TO USE.

1994 ★ USPS goes online with its first public internet site.

2001 ★ USPS forms a business relationship with Federal Express.

2003 ★ USPS forms a business relationship with United Parcel Service.

2005 ★ The volume of First-Class Mail is less than that for other mail, including marketing mail, for the first time.

2006 ★ The Postal Accountability and Enhancement Act is signed into law by President George W. Bush.

2015 ★ Megan Brennan, the first woman postmaster general, takes office; she retires in 2019.

2020 ★ The United States goes under lockdown to help stop the spread of the coronavirus (COVID-19). USPS continues to deliver mail.

★ Many Americans choose to vote using mail-in ballots for the presidential election in November, to avoid catching COVID-19 by standing in line with other people. Cuts to mail service cause alarm. Courts order that USPS operate at full speed, which it does successfully.

2021 ★ Postmaster General Louis DeJoy's strategic plan, "Delivering for America," goes into effect. It creates longer delivery times and cuts in service.

2022 ★ The Postal Service Reform Act is signed by President Joe Biden into law. It cancels USPS's large debt and provides more funds for running USPS.

★ USPS begins delivery of free in-home COVID-19 tests.

NOTES

Full bibliographic information for books cited in Notes can be found in the Selected Bibliography.

Introduction

1 "Vernon O. Lytle": "Baby Boy by Parcel Post," *New York Times*, Jan. 26, 1913, timesmachine.nytimes.com/timesmachine/1913 /01/26/100250414.html.

3 "to establish Post Offices and post Roads": "U.S. Constitution Annotated: Article 1. Legislative Branch; Section VIII," Legal Information Institute, Cornell Law School, law.cornell.edu /constitution-conan/article-1/section-8.

3 By 1801, when the United States: Winifred Gallagher, *How the Post Office Created America* (New York: Penguin, 2016), 34.

3 "[The mail] is to the body politic": Andrew Jackson, "First Annual Message," American Presidency Project, presidency.ucsb.edu /documents/first-annual-message-3.

4 "Here on a sledge made of whalebone": Devin Leonard, *Neither Snow nor Rain: A History of the United States Postal Service* (New York: Grove Press, 2016), 82.

4 "I traveled along a portion": Alexis de Tocqueville, *Democracy in America*, Chapter 17: "Principal Causes Which Tend to Maintain the Democratic Republic of the United States," xroads.virginia.edu /~Hyper/DETOC/1_ch17.htm.

5 516,500 people: Martin Placek, "Number of United States Postal

Service Employees from 2004 to 2021," Statista, May 18, 2022, statista.com/statistics/320262/number-of-usps-employees.

6 "Minorities comprise 52 percent": *United States Postal Service Fiscal Year 2021 Report to Congress*, 13, about.usps.com /what/financials/annual-reports/fy2021.pdf?msclkid =20269dd6c27311ec9b8b3c650a4bc093.

6 "The Postal Service is also a leading employer of veterans": Ibid.

7 "Nothing mortal": Herodotus, *The History of Herodotus*, vol. 4, ed. George Rawlinson (London: John Murray, 1860), 344. See books.google.com/books?id=V3M-AAAAYAAJ&pg=PA344.

9 "I ran into [songwriter] Brian Holland": "Freddie Gorman (1939–2006)," Spectropop, spectropop.com/remembers /FreddieGorman.htm.

10 "There is nothing which is not helped by the Post Office": Hearings Before the Committee on Ways and Means, House of Representatives, on the Revenue Act of 1918 (Washington, DC: Government Printing Office, 1918), 2049. See books.google.com /books?id=cMNCAQAAMAAJ&pg=PA2049.

10 91 percent of Americans: "U.S. Postal Service Tops List Again as Americans' Favorite Government Agency," United States Postal Service, Apr. 25, 2020, about.usps.com/newsroom/national -releases/2020/0415-usps-tops-list-again-as-americans-favorite -government-agency.htm.

1 Expanding with the New Country

14 "That I have not the Propensity to sitting Still": "From Benjamin Franklin to William Strahan, 8 August 1763," Founders Online,

National Archives, founders.archives.gov/documents/Franklin
/01-10-02-0172.

14 riding some 1,780 miles: Ibid.

16 "very bad, Incumbered with Rocks": Gallagher, *How the Post Office Created America*, 16.

19 "The power of establishing post roads": "The Federalist Papers: No. 42," Avalon Project, Yale Law School, avalon.law.yale.edu /18th_century/fed42.asp.

20 Congress simplified postal rates in 1845: "Postmasters' Provisionals, (1845–1847)," National Postal Museum, Smithsonian Institution, postalmuseum.si.edu/exhibition/about-us-stamps /postmasters-provisionals-1845-1847#:~:text=The%20Act%20of %20Congress%20of,rates%20that%20had%20preceded%20it.

23 "In the selection of riders": Gallagher, *How the Post Office Created America*, 55.

25 "celerity, certainty, and security": "What Is a Star Route?," National Postal Museum, Smithsonian Institution, postalmuseum .si.edu/exhibition/networking-a-nation/what-is-a-star-route.

26 "There's a sail in the bow": *The United States Postal Service: An American History*, Publication 100 (Washington, DC: United States Postal Service, 2020), 25.

29 "I can remember no night": Edmund Hope Verney, "An Overland Journey from San Francisco to New York," Good Words, June 1, 1866. See books.google.com/books?id=p35NAAAAYAAJ&pg=PA382.

32 at its beginning, it charged $5: Evan Andrews, "10 Things You May Not Know About the Pony Express," History, June 3, 2016, history. com/news/10-things-you-may-not-know-about-the-pony-express.

33 *"HERE HE COMES!"*: Gallagher, *How the Post Office Created America*, 139–40.

2 Slavery, Civil War, and the Mail

36 "We owe an obligation": Defensor, *The Enemies of the Constitution Discovered; or, An Inquiry into the Origin and Tendency of Popular Violence* (New York: Leavitt, Lord, 1835), 124. See books.google.com /books?id=x1D8IomX1ZQC.

36 "will assuredly not be punished": "Charleston Post Office Break-in, 1835," Records of Rights, National Archives, recordsofrights.org /events/149/charleston-post-office-break-in.

36 "a wicked plan of exciting the Negroes": Leonard, *Neither Snow nor Rain*, 26.

38 "Well, Miss Han": "Letter Writing in America: Civil War Letters," National Postal Museum, Smithsonian Institution, postalmuseum .si.edu/research-articles/letter-writing-in-america/civil-war-letters.

38 "I know that a good cry": "Importance of Mail," U.S. Army Heritage & Education Center, ahec.armywarcollege.edu/exhibits /CivilWarImagery/cheney_mail.cfm.

38 "The mails during the war": "George L. Swett, Postmaster of Portland, Maine," *Portland (Maine) Board of Trade Journal*, 11, no. 5 (Sept. 1898): 36, books.google.com/books?id=rRE -AQAAMAAJ&source=gbs_similarbooks.

39 "We have moved so often": "A Nation Divided: Soldiers' Mail," National Postal Museum, Smithsonian Institution, postalmuseum .si.edu/exhibitions/a-nation-divided/soldiers-mail.

41 "For several months we suffered here": "Depot of Prisoners of War on

Johnson's Island, Ohio: Letters to and from Confederate Prisoners," Johnson's Island Preservation Society, johnsonsisland.org/history-pows/civil-war-era/letters-to-and-from-confederate-prisoners.

43   about 450 letter carriers: Leonard, *Neither Snow nor Rain*, 48.

43   "Everyone understands how great a convenience": "Montgomery Blair: Free Delivery," National Postal Museum, Smithsonian Institution, postalmuseum.si.edu/research-articles/montgomery -blair-blair-steps-in/free-delivery.

43   "Be sure and write quickly": "The Departure of Secesh Women for Richmond," Daily Observations from the Civil War, Jan. 15, 2013, dotcw.com/the-departure-of-secesh-women-for-richmond.

45   nearly eight hundred cities: *The United States Postal Service*, 29.

45   it had restored some 240 mail routes: Ibid., 19.

3 Upgrading the System

50   "informs . . . [us] that eleven years ago": David A. Thompson, *The Mail Is Coming: 100 Years of the Railway Post Office in Minnesota*, Minnesota Historical Society, n.d., 208, collections.mnhs.org /mnhistorymagazine/articles/64/v64i05p206-216.pdf.

50   more than 3,000 railroad clerks: Ibid.

50   By 1930, more than 10,000 trains: *The United States Postal Service*, 22.

50   "On his memory, accuracy, and integrity": "Address Delivered at Michigan's Seventh Annual Convention by Hon. E. T. Bushnell, Chief Clerk to the First-Assistant Postmaster-General," *Postal Clerk* 7, no. 7 (June 1908): 16.

52   Between 1890 and 1905, 142 clerks lost their lives: "The Railway

Mail Service: Wrecks," National Postal Museum, Smithsonian Institution, postalmuseum.si.edu/research-articles/the-railway -mail-service-danger-on-the-rail/wrecks.

52 41 million, about 65 percent of the population: *The United States Postal Service*, 31.

54 forty-four rural routes in twenty-nine states: "Universal Service and the Postal Monopoly: A Brief History," Oct. 2008, about.usps.com/universal-postal-service/universal-service-and -postal-monopoly-history.txt.

54 more than 10,000 petitions: *The United States Postal Service*, 31.

54 8,500 rural carriers: Ibid.

56 "one gloved hand in the severest weather": Ibid, 32.

56 "our mail [delivered] fresh instead of stale": Ibid.

56 "I am more than ever proud": Ibid.

57 More than 500 million Elvis stamps: "America's Most Popular Stamp," Mystic Stamp Company, info.mysticstamp.com/this-day -in-history-january-8-1993.

58 "had become a great university": Gallagher, *How the Post Office Created America*, 210.

59 "We have . . . given first-aid treatment": "Universal Service and the Postal Monopoly."

60 "Express companies extend their business": Ibid.

62 "Supplies for Every Trade and Calling on Earth": Joel Shrock, *The Gilded Age* (Westport, CT: Greenwood Press, 2004), 49.

62 4 million packages: "Universal Service and the Postal Monopoly."

63 "cheapest supply house on earth": Sarah Pruitt, "When the Sears Catalog Sold Everything from Houses to Hubcaps," History,

Oct. 16, 2018, updated Mar. 13, 2019, history.com/news/sears
-catalog-houses-hubcaps.

63 "one-fourth of the entire population": "Universal Service and the
Postal Monopoly."

63 "we will furnish all the material": Pruitt, "When the Sears Catalog
Sold Everything from Houses to Hubcaps."

63 "John Oswald": *New York Times*, Jan. 26, 1913, 4,
timesmachine.nytimes.com/timesmachine/1913/01/26
/100250416.html?pageNumber=1.

64 "live or dead": "The Railway Mail Service: Expansion and Turmoil,
1876–1920," National Postal Museum, Smithsonian Institution,
postalmuseum.si.edu/research-articles/the-railway-mail-service
-history-of-the-service/expansion-and-turmoil-1876-1920.

64 "The babe was weighed, stamped": *Fairmont West Virginian*,
Jan. 12, 1914, from Chronicling America: Historic American
Newspapers, Library of Congress, chroniclingamerica.loc.gov
/lccn/sn86092557/1914-01-12/ed-1/seg-1.

64 "Mrs. E. H. Staley today received": *Bryan Daily Eagle and Pilot*
(Texas), Feb. 3, 1914, from Chronicling America: Historic American
Newspapers, Library of Congress, chroniclingamerica.loc.gov
/lccn/sn86088651/1914-02-03/ed-1/seg-1.

65 "was transported 25 miles": "Live Baby by Parcel Post," *New York
Times*, Feb. 4, 1914, timesmachine.nytimes.com/timesmachine
/1914/02/04/issue.html.

65 Charlotte May Pierstorff: "100 Years of Parcels, Packages, and
Packets, Oh My! The Oddest Parcels," National Postal Museum,
Smithsonian Institution, postalmuseum.si.edu/research-articles

/100-years-of-parcels-packages-and-packets-oh-my/the-oddest
-parcels.

4 Mail Moves Up into the Air . . .

69 *59 seconds:* "1903—The First Flight," Wright Brothers National Memorial, North Carolina, National Park Service, nps.gov/wrbr /learn/historyculture/thefirstflight.htm.

69 *"never forget that the engine may stop":* "Practical Hints on Flying," *Air Service Journal* 2, no. 2 (Jan. 10, 1918): 1.

70 *"I felt I had a thousand friends":* Leonard, *Neither Snow nor Rain*, 106–107.

71 *"I was flying over territory":* Ibid., 107.

72 *33 hours and 20 minutes:* "James H. Knight," Wikiwand, wikiwand.com/en/James_H._Knight.

74 *"The great postal highway":* Gallagher, *How the Post Office Created America*, 221.

76 *"An air-mail sack weighs about 70 pounds":* Leonard, *Neither Snow nor Rain*, 135.

77 *Some 1,500 to 1,800 V-mail:* "Victory Mail: How Did V-Mail Stack Up?," National Postal Museum, Smithsonian Institution, postalmuseum.si.edu/exhibition/victory-mail-introducing-v-mail /how-did-v-mail-stack-up.

78 *Between June 1942 and November 1945:* "V-MAIL IS SPEED MAIL," National World War II Museum, nationalww2museum.org /war/articles/mail-call-v-mail.

78 *almost 5 million pounds:* "Victory Mail: How Did V-Mail Stack Up?"

79   Between 1940 and 1960, the volume of mail: Leonard, *Neither
Snow nor Rain*, 141.

79   by 1966, nearly 18,000 of them: *The United States Postal
Service*, 53.

81   "After hearing that the afternoon mail": Joanne Oppenheim,
*Dear Miss Breed: True Stories of the Japanese American
Incarceration During World War II and a Librarian Who Made
a Difference* (New York: Scholastic, 2006), 75.

81   "They did not know one Japanese name": Ibid., 88.

5 From Post Office Department . . .

85   The Chicago Post Office: *Landmark Designation Report: Old
Chicago Main Post Office Building*," Commission on Chicago
Landmarks, Dec. 7, 2017, 25, 29, Old_Chicago_Main_Post_Office
_Bldg.pdf.

86   "About 1,000 volunteer postal workers": "Backlog of Mail
Jams Post Office in Chicago," *New York Times*, Oct. 10, 1966,
timesmachine.nytimes.com/timesmachine/1966/10/10/issue.html.

86   "At the peak of the crisis in Chicago": *The United States Postal
Service*, 61.

88   In 1945, nearly 38 billion pieces: Ryan Ellis, "The Birth of the
USPS and the Politics of Postal Reform," MIT Press Reader,
thereader.mitpress.mit.edu/birth-of-usps-politics-of-postal-reform.

88   "We are trying to move our mail": "The History and Experience
of African Americans in America's Postal Service: Chicago:
A Postal Shutdown," National Postal Museum, Smithsonian
Institution, postalmuseum.si.edu/research-articles/the-history

-and-experience-of-african-americans-in-america%E2%80%99s
-postal-service-4.

88 The first zip code ever issued: "Where Was the First Zip Code
Issued?," US Global Mail, usglobalmail.com/where-was-the-first
-zip-code-issued.

90 a deficit of more than $1 billion: Ellis, "The Birth of the USPS and
the Politics of Postal Reform."

90 "The reason we went on strike": Philip F. Rubio, *There's Always
Work at the Post Office* (Chapel Hill: University of North Carolina
Press, 2010), 237.

90 pay raise of 4 to 5.4 percent: "The Great 1970 Mail Strike That
Stunned the Country," American Postal Workers Union, Feb. 28,
2017, apwu.org/news/great-1970-mail-strike-stunned-country.

90 150,000 to 200,000 postal workers: Ibid.

91 "A modern economy is sustained": Leonard, *Neither Snow nor
Rain*, 176.

94 How the New USPS Worked: *The United States Postal Service*,
64–65.

101 Nearly 23 million Americans: Figure converted from the
percentage cited in Andrew Perrin and Sara Atske, "7% of Americans
Don't Use the Internet. Who Are They?", Pew Research Center,
Apr. 2, 2021, www.pewresearch.org/fact-tank/2021/04/02
/7-of-americans-dont-use-the-internet-who-are-they.

102 advertised its service in twenty-four languages: Mehrsa
Baradaran, "A Short History of Postal Banking," Slate, Aug. 18, 2014,
slate.com/news-and-politics/2014/08/postal-banking-already-
worked-in-the-usa-and-it-will-work-again.html.

102 In 1915, 70 percent of all deposits: Ibid.

102 Depositors earned 2 percent: postalmuseum.si.edu/collections
/object-spotlight/postal-savings-system.

103 By 1934, postal savings banks held $1.2 billion: Baradaran,
"A Short History of Postal Banking."

6 African Americans in the Post Office

106 "If the inhabitants . . . should deem their letters safe": "The
History and Experience of African Americans in America's
Postal Service: Colonial to Antebellum: The Beginning of
Discrimination," National Postal Museum, Smithsonian Institution,
postalmuseum.si.edu/research-articles/the-history-and
-experience-of-african-americans-in-america%E2%80%99s
-postal-service-0.

107 "If you admitted a negro to be a *man*": Historian, United States
Postal Service, "African American Postal Workers in the 19th
Century," Oct. 2017, 1, about.usps.com/who/profile/history/rtf
/african-american-workers-19thc.rtf.

107 "was generally allowed in the Southern States": "The History
and Experience of African Americans in America's Postal Service:
Colonial to Antebellum."

107 "after the scenes which St. Domingo": Ibid.

109 "After the 1st day of November next": Ibid.

109 The fine for a white person: Philip F. Rubio, *There's Always Work
at the Post Office*, 19.

109 "no person, by reason of color": Ibid., 21.

110 "the first colored man employed about the United States Mail":

Historian, USPS, "African American Postal Workers in the 19th Century," 3.

110 "never lost a day": Ibid.

112 More than three hundred African Americans: Ibid.

116 "rule of three": Rubio, *There's Always Work at the Post Office*, 301n.

118 "comparatively well educated negroes": Historian, United States Postal Service, "African-American Postal Workers in the 20th Century," Feb. 2012, about.usps.com/who/profile/history/african -american-workers-20thc.htm.

119 "It is and should be my consistent policy": Ibid.

119 By 1912, about 4,000 African Americans: Ibid.

120 Burleson "was anxious to segregate": Nancy J. Weiss, "The Negro and the New Freedom: Fighting Wilsonian Segregation," *Political Science Quarterly* 84, no. 1 (Mar. 1969): 64, doi. org/10.2307/2147047.

121 "Mrs. Minnie Cox, Postmistress of Indianola": "The History and Experience of African Americans in America's Postal Service: Minnie M. Cox: A Postmaster's Story," National Postal Museum, Smithsonian Institution, postalmuseum.si.edu/research-articles /the-history-and-experience-of-african-americans-in-america %E2%80%99s-postal-service/minnie.

121 "When the people in the localities": Historian, USPS, "African-American Postal Workers in the 20th Century."

121 He called it "intolerable": "On this Day—Apr[il] 11, 1913: President Wilson Authorizes Segregation Within Federal Government," Equal Justice Initiative, calendar.eji.org/racial-injustice/apr/11.

122   "I regret that I must arise as an American citizen": Rubio, *There's Always Work at the Post Office*, 40.

122   28 percent of clerks and 5 percent of foremen: Historian, USPS, "African-American Postal Workers in the 20th Century."

123   "A city where a Negro": Ibid.

124   In 1959, 66 percent: Ibid.

124   In the early 1960s, Black Americans: Ibid.

125   "It is important to note that most of the women": Rubio, *There's Always Work at the Post Office*, 171.

125   "I was able to raise them": Jeff Brady, "Black Americans Worry Postal Changes Could Disrupt History of Secure Jobs," NPR, Aug. 31, 2020, npr.org/2020/08/31/907062526/black-americans -worry-postal-changes-could-disrupt-history-of-secure-jobs.

7 Women in the Post Office

128   "was driving her mail wagon": Historian, United States Postal Service, "Women Mail Carriers," June 2007, about.usps.com/who /profile/history/pdf/women-carriers.pdf.

129   "was pretty tough sometimes": Ibid.

130   "on at least two routes": "A Century of Progress: Honoring the March Forward of Women Letter Carriers," *Postal Record*, Mar. 2018, 17, www.nalc.org/news/the-postal-record/2018 /march-2018/document/pages-16-21-women.pdf.

130   only ninety-five women: Ibid.

130   "the receipt and dispatch": Historian, United States Postal Service, "Women Postmasters," Feb. 2021, about.usps.com/who /profile/history/pdf/women-postmasters.pdf.

131 "it has not been the practice": Ibid.

132 "At her own risque": "To George Washington from Mary Katherine Goddard, 23 December 1789," Founders Online, National Archives, founders.archives.gov/documents /Washington/05-04-02-0302.

133 "been discharged from her Office": Ibid.

133 "I have uniformly avoided interfering": Ibid.

134 Eight women were listed: Historian, USPS, "Women Postmasters."

135 In 1862, some ten women: "Women in the U.S. Postal System: Postal Women in the Late 19th Century," National Postal Museum, Smithsonian Institution, postalmuseum.si.edu/research-articles /women-in-the-us-postal-system-chapter-1-women-in-postal -history/postal-women-in-0.

136 19 percent of these jobs: Historian, United States Postal Service, "Women of Postal Headquarters," Sept. 2015, about.usps.com /who-we-are/postal-history/women-at-headquarters.pdf.

137 The *Ladies Home Journal* applauded: Kihm Winship, "The Blind Reader," Faithful Readers, Aug. 16, 2016, faithfulreaders.com/2016 /08/16/the-blind-reader.

137 "Tossy Tanner, Tx": Bess Lovejoy, "Patti Lyle Collins, Super-Sleuth of the Dead Letter Office," Mental Floss, Aug. 25, 2015, mentalfloss .com/article/67304/patti-lyle-collins-super-sleuth-dead-letter-office.

137 "Picking up an envelope": Winship, "The Blind Reader."

137 "A letter to a law firm": Ibid.

138 "The women of the Department": Historian, USPS, "Women of Postal Headquarters."

138 "a married woman will not be appointed": 56 Cong. Rec. H9504
(Aug. 24, 1918). See www.govinfo.gov/content/pkg/GPO-CRECB
-1918-pt9-v56/pdf/GPO-CRECB-1918-pt9-v56-29.pdf.

140 "I've done a lot of flying": Adam Lynch, "Hometown Heroine:
Helen Richey," HistoryNet, Mar. 21, 2018, historynet.com
/hometown-heroine-helen-richey.

140 "Katherine Stinson, the aviatrix": "Fad to Fundamental: Airmail
in America: The Stinsons," National Postal Museum, Smithsonian
Institution, postalmuseum.si.edu/exhibition/fad-to-fundamental
-airmail-in-america-airmail-pilot-stories-mail-by-female/the
-stinsons.

141 2.8 percent of jobs: Historian, USPS, "Women of Postal
Headquarters."

141 "She looks and smiles like a runaway schoolgirl": "Katherine
Stinson the Flying Girl: Topics in Chronicling America," Library of
Congress, guides.loc.gov/chronicling-america-katherine-stinson.

142 40 percent of senior management: United States Postal Service,
*Fiscal Year 2020 Annual Report to Congress: An Essential Public
Service*, updated May 14, 2021, 21, about.usps.com/what
/financials/annual-reports/fy2020.pdf.

142 47 percent of postal workers: United States Postal Service, *Fiscal
Year 2020 Annual Report to Congress*, 21.

8 Latinos, Asian Americans, and Native Americans in the Post Office

147 Early Postmasters: Email from Jennifer Lynch, USPS historian
and corporate information services manager, Apr. 19, 2022.

148 118 post offices: Evan Kalish, "Postally Puerto Rico," *Postlandia* (blog), May 30, 2017, blog.evankalish.com/2017/05/postally -puerto-rico.html.

149 225 Latinos serving as postmasters: Email from Jennifer Lynch, Apr. 19, 2022.

149 "Mr. Madrid . . . can neither read nor write": Cameron Blevins, *Paper Trails: The US Post and the Making of the American West* (New York: Oxford University Press, 2021), 155.

150 "he was one of Kennedy's last appointments": Kate Folmar, "Hector Godinez: First Latino Postmaster," *Los Angeles Times*, May 17, 1999, latimes.com/archives/la-xpm-1999-may-17-me-38181- story.html.

151 "news flash of the New York City carrier strike": Philip F. Rubio, *Undelivered: From the Great Postal Strike of 1970 to the Manufactured Crisis of the U.S. Postal Service* (Chapel Hill: University of North Carolina Press, 2020), 65.

152 "we need more Latino employees and managers": Linda B. Benbow, *Sorting Letters, Sorting Lives: Delivering Diversity in the United States Post Office* (Lanham, MD: Lexington Books, 2010), 25.

152 "going to a fiesta": Ibid., 49.

152 In 2003, Latinos made up 7 percent: Ibid., 16.

152 "It's our goal to continue": "U.S. Postal Service Plans to Increase Hiring of Hispanic Workers," *San Antonio Business Journal*, Oct. 10, 2006, bizjournals.com/sanantonio/stories/2006/10/09/daily12.html.

152 17 percent of postal workers: *United States Postal Service Fiscal Year 2021 Report to Congress*, 13.

154   USPS names sixty Asian or Hawaiian postmasters: "Hawaiian Postmasters with Possible Asian or Native Surnames," compiled by USPS, received by email from Jennifer Lynch, USPS historian and corporate information services manager, May 2, 2022.

155   Chu Ching Quong: Ibid.

156   "Lee transformed the face of San Francisco's postal system": "Pelosi Floor Speech on Legislation Naming Lim Poon Lee Post Office in San Francisco," Newsroom, Nancy Pelosi, Speaker of the House, July 21, 2006, speaker.gov/newsroom/pelosi-floor-speech -legislation-naming-lim-poon-lee-post-office-san-francisco.

157   "I was mentored by [a white] manager": Linda B. Benbow, "The Paradoxes of Diversity: Race, Class, and Gender Relations in a Federal Bureaucracy," PhD dissertation, City University of New York, 2006, 167, academicworks.cuny.edu/cgi/viewcontent .cgi?article=4744&context=gc_etds.

157   "Sometimes the whites": Ibid., 154.

157   thirty postmasters and fourteen officers-in-charge: "Postmaster Finder: Postmasters by City," results for "Houston, Texas," United States Postal Service, webpmt.usps.gov/pmt002.cfm.

158   In 2020, Asian Americans represented 7 percent: pewresearch.org/fact-tank/2020/05/14/the-state-of-the-u-s -postal-service-in-8-charts.

158   The number rose to 8.3 percent in 2022: "Commitment to Diversity": in *United States Postal Service Fiscal Year 2021 Annual Report to Congress*, Asian Pacific American Heritage Month, link. usps.com/2022/04/29/asian-pacific-american-heritage-month-2.

159   18.9 million people, in 2019: Abby Budiman and Neil G. Ruiz,

"Asian Americans Are the Fastest-Growing Racial or Ethnic Group in the U.S.," Pew Research Center, Apr. 9, 2021, pewresearch.org /fact-tank/2021/04/09/asian-americans-are-the-fastest-growing -racial-or-ethnic-group-in-the-u-s.

161   White Mountain reservation: Blevins, *Paper Trails*, 44.

162   "an Indian citizen": Ibid., 107.

162   Navajo Steve Begay: Alastair Lee Bitsoi, "First Native American Appointed Postmaster Is Diné," *Navajo Times*, Jan. 24, 2013, navajotimes.com/business/2013/0113/012413pos.php.

162   Native Americans . . . less than 2 percent: "Commitment to Diversity": in *United States Postal Service Fiscal Year 2021 Annual Report to Congress*, 13.

162   "Many homes on reservations": "Vote by Mail in Native Communities," Native American Rights Fund, narf.org /vote-by-mail.

9 U.S. Postal Inspection Service

166   "how to cure hysterics . . . aware of your presence": "Mail-Bag Mysteries," *New York Times*, June 11, 1871, timesmachine.nytimes.com /timesmachine/1871/06/11/issue.html.

167   "The largest business": Ibid.

168   "cases of mail robberies": *The United States Postal Service*, 92.

168   "any scheme or artifice to defraud": Todd E. Molz, "The Mail Fraud Statute: An Argument for Repeal by Implication," *University of Chicago Law Review* 64, no. 3, article 7 (1997): 983, chicagounbound.uchicago.edu/cgi/viewcontent .cgi?article=5639&context=uclrev.

170 $15 million in eight months: Mary Darby, "In Ponzi We Trust,"
Smithsonian, Dec. 1998, smithsonianmag.com/history
/in-ponzi-we-trust-64016168.

172 "The robbers mounted": "Butch Cassidy and the Sundance
Kid Rob a Train, 1899," Eyewitness to History, 1999,
eyewitnesstohistory.com/cassidy.htm.

174 "It's the safest way": Historian, United States Postal Service,
"Hope Diamond Delivered by Mail," Mar. 2002, about.usps.com
/who/profile/history/pdf/hope-diamond.pdf.

174 The postage was $2.44: Nancy Pope, "Delivering the Hope
Diamond," National Postal Museum, Smithsonian Institution,
Nov. 8, 2012, postalmuseum.si.edu/delivering-the-hope-diamond.

175 "I don't believe any of that stuff": Ibid.

176 "At the end of our run": Tim Ratliff, "Railway Mail Service:
Remembering a Time on the Rails," *USPSblog*, Jan. 12, 2018,
uspsblog.com/railway-clerk-remembers.

177 "show up with [her] hat and tie": "Janene Cordon:
A Career of 'Firsts,'" YouTube, July 3, 2018, youtube.com
/watch?v=jnnLWKHZV2I.

177 "No, I want to talk to a real inspector": Ibid.

178 Notable Arrests: "The Biggest Cases of the U.S. Postal Inspection
Service," Universal Postal Union, Nov. 25, 2021, upu.int/en/News
/2021/11/The-biggest-cases-of-the-U-S-Postal-Inspection-Service.

178 Leon Amiel: "*United States v. Amiel*," International
Foundation for Art Research, www.ifar.org/case_summary.
php?docid=1184703560.

178 Ralph Esmerian: "Ralph Esmerian: Rise and Fall of a Jewelry

Connoisseur," Jewelry Loupe, thejewelryloupe.com/rise-and-fall
-of-a-connoisseu.

178   Stephen Bannon: Alex Horton, "The Surprising Mission of the
Postal Service Police Who Arrested Stephen Bannon," *Washington
Post*, Aug. 20, 2020, www.washingtonpost.com/national-security
/2020/08/20/postal-service-police-bannon.

179   "nearly 5,000 arrests": U.S. Postal Inspection Service Case
Management of Arrests," USPS Office of Inspector General,
uspsoig.gov/document/us-postal-inspection-service-case-
management-arrests.

179   "It doesn't matter what the piece of mail is": "Publication 162:
United States Postal Inspection Service: Because the Mail Matters,"
United States Postal Service, PSN 7610-05-000-5085, Feb. 2009,
about.usps.com/publications/pub162/welcome.htm.

10 The Post Office of the Future

182   "more than $5 billion each year: Kevin R. Kosar, *The Postal
Accountability and Enhancement Act: Overview and Issues for
Congress*, Congressional Research Service, Dec. 14, 2009,
sgp.fas.org/crs/misc/R40983.pdf.

182   In 2020, it lost $9.2 billion: David Shepardson, "U.S. Postal
Service Reports $4.9 Billion 2021 Net Loss," Reuters, Nov. 11, 2021,
reuters.com/business/us-postal-service-reports-49-billion-2021
-net-loss-2021-11-10.

183   In a Harris Poll released in June 2020: Annie Prunsky, "The Harris
Poll Releases List of 100 Essential Companies Tied to Corporate
Response to COVID-19 Pandemic," Harris Poll,

June 12, 2021, theharrispoll.com/briefs/the-harris-poll-releases
-list-of-100-essential-companies-tied-to-corporate-response-to
-covid-19-pandemic.

185 "They don't have the money": Jacob Bogage, "Trump Says Postal
Service Needs Money for Mail-in Voting, but He'll Keep Blocking
Funding," *Washington Post*, Aug. 12, 2020, washingtonpost.com
/business/2020/08/12/postal-service-ballots-dejoy.

188 USPS used to send 20 percent: Jacob Bogage, "USPS Is About
to Charge You More for Slower Mail. Here's Why," *Washington Post*,
Oct. 1, 2021, washingtonpost.com/business/2021/10/01/usps
-slowdown-prices-faq.

188 61 percent of First-Class Mail: Ellen Ioanes, "Mail Delays and
Price Hikes Are Coming to USPS. Here's Why," Vox, Oct. 3, 2021,
vox.com/2021/10/3/22707067/usps-mail-slower-more
-expensive-why.

189 What the Postal Service Reform Act of 2022 Calls For: "NALC
Fact Sheet: Postal Service Reform Act (H.R. 3076)," National
Association of Letter Carriers, nalc.org/government-affairs/body
/Postal-Service-Reform-Act-Fact-Sheet-1-1.pdf.

190 "Our country is pretty divided right now": Emily Cochrane,
"Congress Approves Legislation to Return the Postal Service to
Solvency," *New York Times*, Mar. 8, 2022, nytimes.com/2022
/03/08/us/politics/congress-postal-service.html.

Epilogue

191 "Do we really want to ditch": "The Past and Present of the
U.S. Postal Service," *Takeaway*, WNYC Studios, July 26, 2021,

www.wnycstudios.org/podcasts/takeaway/segments/history-and-future-us-postal-service.

192 About 66 million Americans: Letter from Celia Winslow, senior vice president, American Financial Services Association, to Ed Perlmutter, chairman, and Blaine Luetkemeyer, ranking member, U.S. House Subcommittee on Consumer Protection and Financial Institutions, Washington, DC, July 21, 2021, afsaonline.org /wp-content/uploads/2021/07/AFSA-Letter-Unbanked-Hearing -July-2021-1.pdf.

192 "low-cost checking": Press release, "Senators Gillibrand and Sanders Reintroduce Postal Banking Act to Fund United States Postal Service and Provide Basic Financial Services to Underbanked Americans," press release, Kirsten Gillibrand, U.S. Senator for New York, Sept. 17, 2020, gillibrand.senate.gov/news /press/release/senators-gillibrand-and-sanders-reintroduce -postal-banking-act-to-fund-united-states-postal-service-and -provide-basic-financial-services-to-underbanked-americans.

192 It issues money orders—more than $20 billion worth: "Senators Gillibrand and Sanders' Medium Piece: Establish Postal Banking to Provide Equal Financial Opportunity for All," press release, Kirsten Gillibrand, U.S. Senator for New York, Sept. 25, 2020, gillibrand.senate.gov/news/press/release/senators-gillibrand-and -sanders-medium-piece-establish-postal-banking-to-provide -equal-financial-opportunity-for-all.

194 "[The] post office . . . is one of the last threads": Rubio, "The Past and Present of the U.S. Postal Service."

SELECTED BIBLIOGRAPHY

*Indicates books suitable for young readers

Benbow, Linda B. *Sorting Letters, Sorting Lives: Delivering Diversity in the United States Post Office*. Lanham, MD: Lexington Books, 2010.

Blevins, Cameron. *Paper Trails: The US Post and the Making of the American West.* New York: Oxford University Press, 2021.

Carroll, Andrew, ed. *War Letters: Extraordinary Correspondence from American Wars.* New York: Scribner, 2001.

Gallagher, Winifred. *How the Post Office Created America.* New York: Penguin Books, 2016.

Henkin, David M. *The Postal Age: The Emergence of Modern Communications in Nineteenth-Century America.* Chicago: University of Chicago Press, 2006.

John, Richard R. *Spreading the News: The American Postal System from Franklin to Morse.* Cambridge, MA: Harvard University Press, 1995.

Leonard, Devin. *Neither Snow nor Rain: A History of the United States Postal Service.* New York: Grove Press, 2016.

*Lucas, Eileen. *Our Postal System.* Brookfield, CT: Millbrook Press, 1999.

*Murphy, Jim. *The Boys' War: Confederate and Union Soldiers Talk About the Civil War.* New York: Clarion Books, 1990.

*Oppenheim, Joanne. *Dear Miss Breed: True Stories of the Japanese American Incarceration During World War II and a Librarian Who Made a Difference.* New York: Scholastic, 2006.

Rosenberg, Barry, and Catherine Macaulay. *Mavericks of the Sky: The First Daring Pilots of the U.S. Air Mail.* New York: Harper Perennial, 2006.

Rubio, Philip F. *There's Always Work at the Post Office: African American Postal Workers and the Fight for Jobs, Justice, and Equality.* Chapel Hill: University of North Carolina Press, 2010.

———. *Undelivered: From the Great Postal Strike of 1970 to the Manufactured Crisis of the U.S. Postal Service.* Chapel Hill: University of North Carolina Press, 2020.

*Somervill, Barbara A. *The History of the Post Office.* Chanhassen, MN: Child's World, 2006.

United States Postal Service. *An American Postal Portrait: A Photographic Legacy.* New York: HarperResource, 2000.

———. *The United States Postal Service: An American History.* Washington, DC: United States Postal Service, 2020.

*Uphall, Margaret. *The U.S. Postal Service: The History of America's Mail System.* New York: PowerKIDS Press, 2018.

IMAGE CREDITS

ACKNOWLEDGMENTS

No one deserves more thanks for helping to shape and shepherd *Who's Got Mail?* than my editor, Howard Reeves. I am continually grateful for his insight and support. Assistant editor Sara Sproull was a marvel at keeping up with what sometimes seemed like almost daily questions and changes, all of which she handled with grace. This book would not be possible without the incomparable design and production people at Abrams Books for Young Readers: senior managing editor Amy Vreeland; production manager Kathy Lovisolo; design manager Heather Kelly; advisors Peggy Garry and Carolyn Levin; senior vice president and publisher Andrew Smith; and intern Charlotte Perez. Special thanks for his thoroughness to copyeditor David Chesanow, and to Sara Corbett for her splendid design. It beautifully reflects the spirit of the text.

Several people have been especially helpful in providing images and information. Bill Lommel of the National Postal Museum must set a record for the speed with which he replies to a request for a scan. Daniel Piazza, the museum's curator of philately, provided information about stamps and took the wonderful photo of mules delivering mail to the Grand Canyon. Mary Ellen Jensen of Alamy has made the process of obtaining images pleasurable, as has Daniel Geraci of Getty Images. Thanks, too, to Ellen Burling of the Lake Geneva Cruise Line for the delightful photo of dock jumpers.

Special thanks go to postal labor historian and author Philip Rubio, who aided me in the challenging task of finding information about Latinos, Asian Americans, and American Indians in Post Office history. I appreciate his generosity with his time and creative ideas. Jenny Lynch, historian for the U.S. Postal Service gave me invaluable guidance about relatively unknown aspects of postal history.

So many family members and friends supported me through the research and writing of this book and endlessly came up with suggestions to make it richer. Many thanks to Janet Chernela, Mary Glen Chitty, Sara Day, Bob Douglass, Ken Meter, James McCourt, Steve Mount, Nancy Osborne, Stella Richardson, Carla Seaquist, Karen and Ray Skean, Vincent Virga, Peggy Wagner, and Pam and Burt Zurer.

Thanks to my husband, Bob, who may know more about the mail than almost anyone in America after listening to me talk about it for over two years. No one could give me more support or be more patient in reading endless drafts. I am grateful to my daughter Catherine and my daughter-in-law Mary Kate Hurley for their continual belief in the value of my books and the way they cheer me on. Thanks to my son, Nick, a historian of American history, whose knowledge and careful reading made *Who's Got Mail?* a more lucid, concise, and appealing book. And finally, thanks to my granddaughter Lily, who, at this writing, is only four years old, but who inspires me to write for young people and the generations of children to come.

INDEX

Note: Page numbers in *italics* refer to illustrations.